OBSCURITY
in your face

Nancy D. Gosse

Order this book online at www.trafford.com/09-0088
or email orders@trafford.com

Most Trafford titles are also available at major online book retailers.

© Copyright 2009 Nancy D. Gosse.

All rights reserved. No part of this publication may be reproduced, stored in a retrieval system, or transmitted, in any form or by any means, electronic, mechanical, photocopying, recording, or otherwise, without the written prior permission of the author.

Book/Cover design by Sue Impey, Design Desktop Publications Inc.

Note for Librarians: A cataloguing record for this book is available from Library and Archives Canada at www.collectionscanada.ca/amicus/index-e.html

Printed in Victoria, BC, Canada.

ISBN: 978-1-4269-0244-4

We at Trafford believe that it is the responsibility of us all, as both individuals and corporations, to make choices that are environmentally and socially sound. You, in turn, are supporting this responsible conduct each time you purchase a Trafford book, or make use of our publishing services. To find out how you are helping, please visit www.trafford.com/responsiblepublishing.html

Our mission is to efficiently provide the world's finest, most comprehensive book publishing service, enabling every author to experience success. To find out how to publish your book, your way, and have it available worldwide, visit us online at www.trafford.com/10510

Trafford PUBLISHING

www.trafford.com

North America & International
toll-free: 1 888 232 4444 (USA & Canada)
phone: 250 383 6864 ♦ fax: 250 383 6804
email: info@trafford.com

The United Kingdom & Europe
phone: +44 (0)1865 487 395 ♦ local rate: 0845 230 9601
facsimile: +44 (0)1865 481 507 ♦ email: info.uk@trafford.com

10 9 8 7 6 5 4 3 2

This book is dedicated first and foremost to
the Great Spirit of All That Is.
Thank you for my Being.

I also dedicate this book to my mother,
to honour the courageous journey she is beginning
into her own heart.

Obscurity ~ n. the quality or condition of being obscure.

Obscure ~ adj. 1. lacking light; dim; dark; murky.
    2. not easily perceived; not clear or distinct; faint or undefined.
    3. not well-known.

Contents

Introduction vii

A Child of the Woods. 1

Forgotten Innocence. 15

Pandora's Box 23

An Empty Dream. 33

Soul Encounter. 40

Awakening the Vision 54

A Whole New World 59

Whatever it Takes. 76

And the Angels Sang 80

A Lesson in Integrity 87

The End of the Beginning .92

Epilogue. 96

Reference List 98

Introduction

I have not always been confident in the sense of who I am and in many ways I'm still not. Yet I find myself taking a big leap of faith, embarking on an adventure in which my life is left wide open. There is the recognition somewhere inside me of an inner voice, a deep purpose to help others; to be the teacher and the student at the same time. Driven by some inner call that many could not possibly understand and many that don't really want to understand, I share this story because there are those who will understand. It is for those people that I am writing this story.

It seems that this story has taken on a life of it's own since the time I first felt that seed planted in my imagination. At the age of 15 with some sense of certainty, I knew that a book about my life would be written. A lady by the name of Jean Houston was giving a talk in 2002 at a Psychic Children's Conference. She stated, "Imagination inspires the imaginal". I suppose that's really what this story is about…a journey into the imaginal.

The title of this story, **Obscurity in Your Face,** came to me a few years ago, long before there were any words to go with it. I wasn't quite sure what it was saying but it felt like an apt description of a life that was hanging out there yet completely shrouded in uncertainty. Now I can relate to this title in a much deeper way, in recognition of the search for spiritual truths that are right there inside of us all along. We simply need to let go of all the obscure details and allow the light of truth to shine forth from who we really are.

As I describe my experiences and weave the threads of my perceptions through this story, it becomes clear that it is really a story that everyone can relate to in some way. Many of us are afraid to speak of those unmentionable thoughts and feelings we carry because someone might find it objectionable. The thing is, I feel the need to speak of what's in my heart regardless of what anyone might think. I have tried not to get too bogged down in details, because the truth isn't really found in the details. The truth is more in the energy of the experiences. By the same token, I have altered some names and some of the details in order to protect the privacy of those involved because my perceptions of this story really has no influence on how others may have perceived it. This writing comes from my feeling and my experience.

It is difficult to try to tell this story in a smooth flow of events because my life experience thus far has been anything but smooth. I have included various writings from journal entries and poems that I've written since childhood so that you might have a sense of the emotions that flowed through the events. It is my hope that this story will, in some way, offer comfort, guidance, and recognition to all of you who feel as I did, that you are living an obscure life while truth is staring you in the face.

Chapter One

Child of the Woods

Childhood seems like the logical place to start telling the story of my awakening. It was as a child that I danced with the fairies in the woods, lay on beds of ferns, and climbed high into the trees to feel the rush of being part of it all, the queen of my castle. It was a magical time of bearing witness to the splendor of the awesome creations of this intricate, complex, and splendid world around us. It was a time of feeling suffocated as I stumbled blindly through a maze of illusory dreams. Painful lessons left me struggling to make amends between the entrapments of the world being presented and the pull of another more intriguing existence. When I didn't want to look at the world around me or feel the unhappiness that came with it, my invisible friends guided me through, entertained me in conversation and even up to the age of twelve, enticed me to look over my shoulder and maintain my awareness of something beyond what most could perceive.

Sure, I had the pleasures of typical childhood with birthday parties, games on the playground, camping in summer, fishing on the river with my bamboo pole, but I always felt a melancholy that as a child I could not name. The continuous call of adventure into a magical unseen world lured me from having to experience the tragedies of the world. I was an adventurer, at least in my mind. On summer mornings, I would pack a lunch with a stick through my bundle, just like Huck Finn, and would head off to my day of adventure. When I wasn't engaged in games of make believe with my friends, I would be spending hours sitting by the waters edge, dangling my feet in the cool water, watching how the sun reflected off the beads of water or noticing how the plants in the pond's bottom wavered with the current of water rushing past. The young tadpoles with tiny legs starting to dangle from their sides fascinated me. Wouldn't it be so cool if we could just decide to sprout new legs, or wings, and just travel into the abyss of some undiscovered destiny?

The woods always spoke to me as I walked through to breathe in the dankness of the mosses clinging to the trees and listening for the crackling of twigs, scurrying critters, or whispers of breezes that I always imagined to be the woodland fairies. It seems that I was a child waiting for something, some unknown magical adventure.

Other than that, my childhood was typical of any other child's. My days were spent twiddling with toys and gadgets, trying to be a great inventor, builder, or homemaker. Many rainbows would grow from the end of my turpentine twigs dragged through the mud puddles. Didn't all kids playing with turpentine rainbows imagine falling into those rainbows and getting swept up in the arms of a beam of light? Thinking back to that time, I question how I could have ever allowed myself to drift away from it. How could such intense connection to the magnificence and utter joyfulness of life ever be forgotten? Come to think of it, I would always be jolted back to reality when some adult would dash my dreams of being in a magical world by pointing out the obvious fact that I was running along the trenches of a newly dug septic field, or messing up my neighbor's yard with tree branches. Little did they know that these branches concealed the portal to my kingdom.

I asked different people in my family to describe me as a child. It was always pretty much the same response. I was a quiet, reserved, pleasant child with rosy cheeks, bright but dark eyes, and always had a smile on my face. I found that a little odd, considering how much sorrow hung over me like a dark, ominous cloud throughout my life. Why wouldn't that joy remain with me? Where did it start to go wrong? Maybe it was when I learned to walk, or rather first ran.

Mom had told me how one day I was up on the bed and became very unsettled and squirmy, which she recalled as being very unusual for me. For some reason I needed to get free. She put me down on the floor to stand with a hand holding on to my safety. There was some hesitation and then one small step, then another, and then I just started running, laughing in pure glee at the discovery of what I could do. Apparently those first few steps turned into a marathon, running back and forth several times. Was I running from something, or just too eager to move toward what was waiting? I think about that now and wonder how it fits for me as an adult. I've always felt that I am very indecisive, and it takes me a long time to finally make a decision about something. However, once I know inside my heart that something is right, I am very focused and committed and give it my all. When my time has come, nothing holds me back.

Then again, running blindly and too excitedly has run me right into many brick walls and humiliating experiences. These experiences served me well to help me grow into recognizing the truth of who I am.

Another example of my childhood sense of endowment came with a story about receiving treats. Mom had been opening a bag of candy to pass around. She asked all of us kids who wanted some and they gathered around. Meanwhile, I came running with my hand out saying "me, me, me". It's kind of a funny story to me, in reflection of how in tune I was with my own wants, and didn't hesitate to reach out and demand it as if I had some inner knowing that I wanted it and I deserved to have it. I've since learned that those were my very first words. My sister remarked how there's usually a little contest over getting a child to say either "mom" or "da" as the first word, but instead it was "me, me, me". I suppose even as a wee thing I somehow knew the gifts of abundance that was inherent in God's creation. Somewhere along the way into adulthood I had forgotten how to be so clear on recognizing my own wants and had willingly put them aside for other people. At some point in time, I had decided that I was not as important.

My childhood history was fairly typical, aside from my woodland adventures with the fairies. My parents had started dating as teenagers. My dad was a tall, handsome, blue-eyed army man. My mom was a dark-eyed, fun-loving spirit and a bit of a handfull according to what her sisters told me. She really liked to have fun and be with her friends. Like many girls in love, she would sneak out her bedroom window to be with her man. My parents were married, as seemed appropriate, since my mom had become pregnant. There was considerable pressure to do the right thing and from what I have been told, there was a letter from my grandmother urging my father to be a proper gentleman. I've often wondered how different things might have looked if they hadn't given in to that pressure.

Five other children, all about a year apart, followed this first-born, whom they named Doug. My brother, Alec, was next. Then the girls arrived. First it was Dana, then Marsha, and Rebecca. All of these children were born approximately a year apart. I would come along four years later. It became a little bit of a joke amongst us that mom and dad must have had some big spat before making up to have me. As it turns out, that theory was pretty accurate. They were split up for a period of time and my dad had left the province. Thankfully, my presence was required, and so they came together again to bring me into the world. Even now the details of what really happened during that time are sketchy. Many times in my life, I had wished they hadn't reunited because then I wouldn't have been born and have to live a life of feeling completely invisible. Isn't it ironic that my life would take such a turn, to come from a place of hurting so much because of feeling invisible only to find myself striving to be invisible and without identity, melding into Oneness of the universe?

We lived in a small house and all the girls had to share the same room, while the two boys shared the other room. We weren't a wealthy family but my parents worked hard, at least my mom did. My dad dropped out of the army in order to stay home with his family. In the early years of their marriage, he worked with a government construction company. That soon fell to the wayside and he picked up income from make-work projects and then drew unemployment to live on. Eventually the drinking got out of hand and he was being picked up a number of times for impaired driving. My mother started working at the local fish plant when I was around five years old. The smell of the plant carried home on her clothes was terrible. I could never understand how she could bear working in that smell. It was very difficult work, especially when she'd then have to come home and scrub her aprons for hours while tending to all of us. She kept it up for years to support her family, and I suppose it provided an escape from the turmoil in her life. It was easy to not have to think too much with conveyor belts spewing out fish. Her work was driven by necessity of ego convincing her that this was the only way, that in order to have anything she would darn well earn it through hard work. Such is the message of my healing journey; to learn to heal from the false belief that I am somehow at fault, unworthy, and the only way to redeem myself as a sinner was to pay my penance.

I remember seeing a photograph once that one of us took of mom after she'd come home from work. She was still in her work clothes, too exhausted to move. She'd sat down in the chair with her arms resting on the back of it, hands under her chin. She had fallen fast asleep sitting up in that chair. The image of that is still etched in my memory as an example of the weariness and utter exhaustion she lived with. More than that, it shows me the belief many of us carry that as sinful human beings, we are forced to wear ourselves down in order to repent for having separated ourselves from God. I understand now that this is a trap that ego has placed in front of us to keep us toiling on an endless cycle of self-depreciation.

My mother was an attractive woman and when she was first married, fairly slim. After having so many babies and toiling away, however, she had gained some weight and started to look worn. As a child I didn't fully appreciate what she was doing for her family, or the role she was playing in helping me to understand the lessons of forgiveness. Like most kids, it just mattered that she came home at the end of the day and tended to our needs. I may not have seen it then, but I can look back now and see how hard she worked her whole life. She was always trying, even though she didn't always succeed. She often used the expression, that she was "taking two steps forward and one step back". The so-called curse of bad fortune seemed to be a theme cloud that hung over her, and later it became one that I too willingly adopted.

As for my father, well, he often disappeared into the background. When my father was around, he kept us entertained with his inventions. I really don't recall him working too much, except for the work he created for himself around the house, and odd jobs here and there. Although, I do remember feeling a great deal of pride over a beautiful fireplace that he had built in his friend's house, and every time we drove to St. John's, I would beam over the Queen Elizabeth ll Library that he was involved in constructing. In my child's innocence, my dad may as well have been a famous Master Builder.

In later years, I would begin to understand that he had his conflicts with his father-in-law over providing properly for his family. His escape was into his bottle and his drinking buddies. He spent a great deal of time fiddling with cars, hauling wood, and he'd always be coming up some sort of scheme for how to get things done. We never knew what to expect from him next. I suppose it seemed exciting from the perspective of a kid who was somewhat oblivious to his faults.

He was a quiet man for the most part, but when he had to raise his voice to be stern, we knew better than to go against him. He was a thinker; the quiet one who stood back, took mental notes, and when he spoke, he did so with conviction. I remember one day that mom and dad got into a disagreement. I don't recall exactly how it started but it seemed to revolve around me having decided to not go to Sunday school that day. Maybe mom was trying to get some back up from dad to convince me why it was so important to always go to Sunday school. I just stood by the window observing my first lost teeth sitting in a glass of water on the window ledge. Whoever came up with the idea of putting teeth in a glass of water for the tooth fairy anyway? Seems like such a bizarre custom. I was completely tuned out from the debate, lost in the little bubbles forming on the side of the glass, thinking about the hard work that went into growing those teeth and hoping to get some decent money from the Tooth Fairy.

Mom had made some kind of remark about dad not being a churchgoer, and not setting an example. He took it all in, and then he took his turn to let mom have it. He started quoting from the bible and running on about the principles of being a Christian; that one doesn't have to be churchgoer to be a decent human being. I don't really know what it was about that exchange, but I remember feeling pride in my dad that day. Perhaps the pride came from him showing me a glimpse of how someone can be misjudged by appearances; how humans run much deeper than they sometimes allow others to see.

At the time, it didn't seem like such a big deal that dad was a drinker because he was not the messy kind of drunk. He always had a bottle of beer around, or have his buddies at the kitchen table to share a few beers. I can laugh now at the many attempts for homebrew and the numerous five-gallon buckets warming by the stove. Still, he was a dad who knew how to have fun with us and he still managed to stand up in defense of the wrongs going on around him. He was always making up little games or building quirky toys that he'd design. He provided us with the entertainment and laughs that mom was never able to; maybe because she was so tired from her work or maybe she just didn't know how. It seemed like it often caused arguments. If it wasn't us kids getting into trouble, it would be dad getting yelled at for getting us all riled up when mom needed us to be serious.

There were times, though, that my parents would have fun together. There was a radio play that used to come on all the time. Mom and dad would often act it out for us. We never grew tired of hearing it. Then there were times that their friends would visit from down the shore. They would gather around telling jokes and stories, or dad would get dressed up in some ridiculous outfit and put on a show. For me, these became a cherished memory of the few times mom and dad really seemed together.

As for us kids, I suppose we were like any other kids. My brothers were always getting into scrapes or concocting schemes of some sort. Dana was usually involved in the schemes with the boys. She was tough and adventurous. I learned to look up to her as my protector. Come to think of it, she was sort of the protector of all us girls. She would always step in to break up the fights or look out for us at school when others were giving us a hard time. I always admired the way she could stand up for herself and take no bull from anyone. She was also very sharp and quick-witted, which I think in some ways, is where I got my sense of humor.

My oldest brother, Doug, left home when I was still young. With a ten-year age gap, we were not relating much to each other anyhow. I just always thought of him as the one who left home to go out and find himself in the big city. It was kind of a cool to think about the idea of going off in search for a life. He was very smart, among the brightest in his class, but he always seemed to struggle with a social life. As much as I can remember, he always seemed to rely on the company of my other brother to include him in things going on. Maybe that was one of the reasons he decided to head out on his own. Maybe he needed to find out who he really was. It seems kind of sad that years later he would return home with nothing much to show except for broken relationships, a weary heart, and trodden esteem. He's often been described like a lost puppy. That's Doug…loyal, kind-hearted and very much still momma's boy, even though he appears at times to resent playing this role but feeling powerless to change it.

Before Doug left he brought to our family something that would become a cherished force, our beloved family dog. Doug had gone up to visit his friend whose dog had puppies. He had called home to ask mom permission to bring one home, but of course, the answer was a resounding no. We had enough animals running about as it was, with hens and chickens and any number of cats around the door, not to mention the many mice in our house. At one point we even had a horse. That didn't last long though, because the horse turned out to be lousy and no one could go near it even to pet it.

Anyway, Doug came strolling in the back door with his arm tucked in under his coat. Mom spied him and immediately caught up on his game. She knew he was trying to sneak this little puppy in. He held out his hand and placed this pudgy little ball of tan colored wrinkles into mom's arms. One look into these chocolate eyes that held the power to soften the hardest resolve, and mom was done for. Doug displayed his characteristic wide grin telling mom he just had to bring this little one home because he knew that as soon as mom saw it, she would agree to give it a home with us.

The little puppy was given the name Ginger and although she was always known as Doug's dog, she had very much become the family treasure. Even when years had passed between Doug's visits home, Ginger would go running up with her tail wagging excitedly in recognition of the gentle, kind master that had brought her home. Like the rest of us, Ginger became part of the games, the tricks, and was sometimes even the central character in our adventures. She was with us for almost fifteen years, a silent and dedicated little creature who despite the conflict and turmoil stood by us and offered her little paw and a lick on our cheek to remind us of her love.

Alec was the only boy left at home once Doug moved out. He also became my protector, of sorts. He was always the cool dude. He was popular and spent a great deal of time hanging out at the snack bar or on the go with his friends. He was such a likeable guy, always with a joke or a trick to get us laughing, and even though he caused some fights, he would be quick to step in to defend us too. Even as a child, I remember always looking up to him and seeing how he made his own way without relying on others too much. He had a carefree approach to life, never seemed to take things too seriously. Alec could also be such a bully and so mean when he wanted to. Still, underneath the toughness he had a gentle way about him. When he started bringing girl friends home, he always included me and made me feel special as his cherished little sis. I remember crying at his wedding, overwhelmed with the feeling that my brother was making a life of his own now, leaving us behind. I was around 11 years old at the time, and I think it was the first real glimpse at how life was changing. It was here where we would all have our first and last family photo taken. Not too long afterwards, our family would start crumbling apart.

Life with my sisters was a mixed bag of jealousy and admiration. They always seemed to doing things that were more interesting, maybe because they were four years older than me and could do more. The two oldest, Dana and Marsha, were already into their late teens and doing more independent things. I remember always spending a lot of time with Dana. She looked out for me, and she became almost like a mother, even getting up early to have me washed and dressed before the others were up. I felt proud being the center of attention among her friends, especially when she'd brought me to the snack bar one day and I got to sit up on the stool and receive treats while watching everyone playing pool or pin-ball. I think she got into big trouble for that one. A snack bar was no place for a kid my age.

Rebecca was closer to my own age and I spent a lot of time hanging out with her friends, sometimes at their displeasure. I remember mom always encouraging Rebecca to include me because the others weren't around. We had a lot of fun together. She became more like a friend than a sister, at least until I got older and found my own friends. We played our games of pretend and inspired each other's imagination. No matter how much we argued we'd always end up laughing our heads off with our own silly games.

My sisters once told me a story about one of the tricks they played on me. I had been chasing them around outside my cousin's house. They kept leading me around in circles around this house. There was a big rock between the house and the fence that I had to climb each time to stay on the path around to the front of the house. I had to work hard at it because still being so young, my legs were still very short to be trying to climb over this rock, but persistence paid off. At some point, Marsha and my cousin had snuck inside the house. They watched from the window as I continued to run circles around the house to catch up to them. I don't know how many times I had circled around, each time having to climb up over this rock again. It reminded me of my innocence, naiveté, and willingness to be led, at least until I grew so tired of running circles that I would stop. I carried some of this quality into my adulthood, sometimes to my own detriment.

It was intriguing to watch my older sisters going through their rituals of growing up, coming of age, discovering boys, wearing make-up, finding just the right outfit, complaining about how they looked. Not Dana though. She was always more natural, practical, and opted for comfortable style, very attractive in her own right. She never bought into the real girly things. I remember her teasing Marsha a lot about the amount of make-up she wore, even stopping her from going out sometimes until she toned down her look. She was looking out for her, trying to help Marsha from getting caught up in the trap of drawing the wrong kind of attention. Marsha was very sensitive to the opinions of others and she worked hard at being accepted. She had been bullied and taunted a great deal in school, as well as Rebecca. Both Marsha and Rebecca were very quiet and passive. Dana always watched out for them. Rebecca never seemed to buy into that image thing either. I always saw her as being more self-assured even through the difficult times that would lie ahead of her.

I spent my days playing outside with friends, never one to stay inside for too long. We made up games to play in the field behind my house, created a baseball team, and played Frisbee. In summer, we would chase the wild horses that came to the field, trying for a chance to ride bareback on this untamed beast. We would often go out to the harbor to watch for the pothead whales, head off with our buckets for blueberry picking, and build forts in the back woods with Dad's lumber. I wanted to so much to build a private space like my big brother's cabin where I could escape to when I wanted to be alone. This didn't get too far though when dad discovered that his new lumber was disappearing. My dream castle dismantled pretty quickly.

Then there were the sweet leaves we'd pick from the back garden. I don't know how these edible delights were ever discovered but they were almost an addiction. We'd pick bowls full of them and we all enjoyed them. Sometimes dad would boil up dandelion leaves too and we'd eat them with our boiled potatoes. One day dad took me down to the back woods to get some turpentine off the trees and showed me how we could chew on it like gum. It was exciting to me to see the gifts of the woods and again delighted in my dad's wisdom about things.

Thunderstorms were always exciting and we brave souls couldn't wait for a good downpour to go swim in the pond. The whole lot of us would pile into the truck, even Ginger, and we'd head off down the road. The water was always so warm during rainstorms, but the heavy raindrops certainly stung our backs as we ran for cover to the truck. In winter we stayed out sledding until late in the evening and then gathered around the wood stove to share hot chocolate until getting sleepy enough to go to bed. Those were our family rituals, the events that brought so much joy in simply being together having fun.

At Halloween we had loads of fun, too. The tricksters that we all were, we would dress up in our costumes, go around the block, and then come home to change into a new outfit and go again. After the second or third round, our neighbors were catching up on our trick. It was just as well; we had already collected about three or four garbage bags of treats, enough to sustain any army. I remember one Halloween dressing up as a member of the heavy metal band, *Kiss*. I wanted to be "Star Child". I don't recall ever really listening to the music of this band, not sure I ever wanted to, but something about being a star child really appealed to me. My favorite jacket to wear was a silver-colored jacket belonging to Rebecca. Eventually, I whined enough about it that it became mine for keeps. It bore the label "Star Captain". Wearing it somehow made me feel important.

Another memory that stood out clearly was what I call my "Chicken Little" adventure when I seriously thought the sky was going to fall on our heads. I had been skating on the marsh. It used to fill up with the bog water and when it froze, it provided a glistening smooth skating arena for a future figure skating champion to glide across. The image of that smooth sheet of ice, glistening from the reflected colors of the evening sky remains fresh in my mind. This one particular evening as the sky started to glow in an orange-pink color from the setting sun; I looked up and saw something in the sky. It was mesmerizing. It looked like a little blue ball with flames of yellow, red, and orange trailing behind it. For a moment, fear gripped me. What was this? Was it going to crash to the earth? Did this mean the end of the world, like they had sometimes heard about on TV? In spite of the fear, I couldn't help but be drawn into the magnificence and vibrant colors of this thing.

After some time of wondering what the heck to do, run home, or duck for cover, I decided that it didn't matter. If I were going to die or be sucked up by some alien, then I would at least fully enjoy my moment as a star on ice. I continued skating until growing tired, figuring out by now that the world probably wasn't about to end. An old truck cap imbedded in the ice served as a bench to sit on while taking off my skates to put my boots back on. It's always such a good feeling to tired feet to have them nestled back inside boots to walk level on the ground. Once again the beautiful image of the sky drew me in. I can laugh now at my own silliness for thinking of such potential disaster, but I recall the feeling of being happy to be alive after avoiding such disaster.

It would later be talked about on TV that the object in the sky was Haley's Comet. This was quite an historical event because it was the closest this comet had ever come to the earth's atmosphere to be seen with the naked eye. At the time, this important fact didn't matter much to me. Even now, I suppose it doesn't really matter that much. I am only too thankful to have the memory of that sky and the feelings that were etched into my heart.

As the youngest in the family, I seemed to get a little bit of both ends, envied for being spoiled but was also protected a great deal by my siblings. We had our disagreements and certainly had our share of fights. Still, through it all, there was a bond between us. Even with all the fighting, we found moments of sheer joy together, laughing so hard that our sides split. We shared our dreams of stardom and often gathered around Marsha's tape recorder and sang our songs as if being presented to the world for a great debut.

I sang my Sunday school songs of Jesus' love bubbling in my soul and about the devil never leaving if your heart is filled with glue. The song actually spoke of a heart filled with gloom but in my ears, it sounded like glue so this is what I sang. Rebecca, in her sweet, quiet manner sang about knowing a place of beauty and repose, where she could dream of beauty to receive and knowing that God made this place for her. Marsha and our cousin sang about coming of age. Mom even had her turn at stardom. She would always be singing her songs of salvation while doing her work around the house. One verse, in particular, seemed to resonate with a theme of God being a rescuer from life's ocean and serving as an anchor in the storms. Dana, as the oldest girl, didn't participate as much in our games and was busy with her own friends. She seemed always vigilant to right the wrongs and became rebellious in many ways to what was happening around us. Through the years we got each other into trouble but we also protected each other. We became so closely knit into each other's world, just as many siblings do, especially those who are going through the trials of a family being slowly torn apart.

Marsha was the middle child and she seemed to be the one who always tried to maintain a sense of family togetherness through collecting our songs and gathering the family photos. Even now, she holds on to scraps of memories, trying to keep together an image of family. A few years back, she had made copies of our song recordings from her old tape recorder. It's a cherished memento of our childhood days together.

I took comfort sometimes lying on top of my bed in my room. Marsha and I shared a bunk bed that my dad had put together using two old metal bed frames. It was a great bed and so comfortable to lie in. I had the top bunk and loved to hang down from the side and sometimes grab on to spin out over to land on the floor, like a trapeze artist. Sometimes at night when we were settling into bed to sleep, I would hang my head down over with my long hair flying about and I would speak to my sister Marsha, imitating the voice of Reagan from *The Exorcist*. It drove Marsha bonkers and really gave her the creeps. She'd kick at the bottom of the mattress underneath me to try to get me to stop. My fun got thwarted quickly when the scolding came for teasing her so much and preventing her from being able to sleep. Every time she'd close her eyes she'd see Reagan coming to get her.

In a room with two sisters, it was a rare treat to be able to lay back on my bed alone and enjoy the quiet space. Sometimes I would drift into my imaginary world, staring at the ceiling or looking out the window into my aunt's beautiful garden next door. This was a garden where I would spend hours crawling through the long grass to create paths and pretend to be on some wild adventure. I remember one sunny afternoon lying back on my bed, again admiring the roses on the trees of her garden, getting ready to drift into a nice nap. I looked at the way the sunshine was streaming in through the window, leaving an image on the floor. The dust particles floating around in the sunbeams seemed to glitter, like fairy dust, and again invited me into a world of make-believe. I danced in those particles, with my magical fairy friends, and was carried away into imagination.

A visit to the garden next door became a daily ritual to hear my aunt tell stories. She always seemed to know who it was by the way the back screen door creaked open and quietly closed behind me. Her house always intrigued me because it seemed mysterious. There was a narrow hallway leading into the kitchen, with several rooms off this hallway. Behind her kitchen was a door leading to somewhere I had never seen. It seemed like a creepy yet appealing entry into somewhere unknown. There were times when I entered her back porch that I would hesitate to go inside because something about the gloomy hallway felt a little scary to me. Sometimes I wouldn't go inside at all and just sit on her back step admiring the garden until someone came along to invite me inside. She would always hear me come in though, and called out from the kitchen. Then she would smile and reach out her arms to say, "well, my goodness, look who's come to share their smile with me today".

Sometimes she scared me a little because she was getting so old. She had so many wrinkles and her body was becoming frail. Still, her eyes sparkled with pure joy of living. When she was younger, she walked with me in her cherished garden to check on her flowers. She would explain things to me; share her knowledge of her garden and of the birds and butterflies that visited. Sometimes when we were sitting in her kitchen, a little bird would flutter up to the window and catch our attention. No matter what she was doing, she would always stop to admire the little bird. That's where I first learned to truly appreciate nature. She had become somewhat of a legend in our town and her garden was a local hot spot where all kinds of people would flock to have wedding photos and family gatherings.

She was so central to our lives, having lived next door to us all through our growing up. In later years, Dana's children would visit her daily as I did as a child. She served up the same comforts and the same dose of love that she'd always given to me. She would live to be one hundred and three and was a great testimony to the beauty of being fully present to each moment of your life. Boy, to sit with her now and hear her stories… what an adventure that would be.

When I reflect on where my path has taken me, my childhood still holds a real sense of wonderment. For many years I tried to forget the sadness and the pain that came with it, but in so doing, the joyousness was also forgotten. As adults, my siblings and I have often joked about our hillbilly days and the scrapes we'd gotten into. We can gather for hours to talk and laugh and cry for what our lives were like. With such an age gap between my siblings, there were not so many tales that included me. Most of them had already moved on by the time I was old enough. Still, there are so many instances of deep wisdom and sheer joy reflected in my childhood. Only now can I realize the light that carried through it all.

Life as we knew it changed pretty quickly, seemingly overnight. I remember hearing a huge argument between my parents, not unlike other arguments that occurred over the years, but this was different. This one came on the heels of some woman I didn't know tearing into the house one day to confront my dad with accusations and pleading with him to keep his wife away from her husband. The details of how the event unfolded are kind of a blur now but I do remember that the next few days were in complete upheaval. It came down to a choice between living with my mother and staying in the house with my father. Part of me wanted to stay to still feel the way I used to when I was daddy's girl.

When I was younger, maybe in grade four, I remember walking home from school after a snow storm. The wind was howling and snow blew fiercely across my face cutting off my breath to the point that I was sure death would claim me. A back route behind the field to the house seemed to promise getting me out of the wind and cold. Unfortunately the snow was deeper, and several times I got stuck barely able to free my feet to walk. When I finally did get home, utterly exhausted and chilled, dad pulled over a chair and took me up into his arms. He sat with me in front of the wood stove to help me thaw out. He had even warmed her favorite slippers on the stove. They got scorched a little, but it didn't matter much because the warmth they offered was too inviting. As I sat there huddled in his arms, the feeling of warmth and safety enveloped me. It was the only clear memory I have of ever feeling perfectly safe and loved.

I also remember in grade three when I had to write a poem for homework. My dad sat with me and helped me write a poem about my kitten. I vaguely remember it now, but what stands out is the fact that my dad was patient and kind and willing to take the time to help. I don't hear many stories these days about fathers taking the time to help their kids write a poem. What we wrote went something like this...

My kitten lies on my lap
whenever she wants to take a nap.
And when I smooth down her fur
My little kitten starts to purr.
Playful is my little kitten
With fingers, hands, even mittens,
But a ball on a string
is her most favorite thing.

Years later, faced with having to choose between my parents, I realized that it no longer fit for me to be daddy's girl. His affections towards me became questionable and uncomfortable. When I think back to those early years, I find it a little bizarre that my memories of feeling most safe and those of feeling most uncomfortably vulnerable were with the same person. It was this confusion that would lead me through years of guilt, anger, and frustration for loving someone so much yet fearing them. He used to look at me and watch me in a way that didn't really feel right. My mother would get impatient with me, trying to get me dressed or ready to take a bath. It was the earliest memory of being told that my feelings didn't count. That was the beginning of a lifetime of placing greater value on opinions outside of me. I can still see the image of my father standing in the crack of the bathroom door, watching me. I still remember how it made me feel icky and invisible while my mother hushed me for being silly.

Chapter Two
Forgotten Innocence

Over the next few years, I would be witness to many of the sad choices people make in order to be loved. From this place of observing and internalizing everything going on around me, I felt removed from my own existence. I guess I was like my father, quietly taking mental notes of what was unfolding around me. The impact of our broken family was starting to take its toll. As an adolescent, I was deeply depressed and felt lost in a world that couldn't be described. It was extremely painful to try to make friends with anyone. I felt ugly, stupid, and branded in some invisible way that repelled people from me. On the outside, people saw me as pretty with my long dark hair and rosy cheeks, but on the inside was a little girl shrinking away. I hated my body and felt so completely naked, like everyone who looked at me could look straight through me, especially men. I'm convinced that some of them actually did. I had lots of reasons not to trust any man.

At age fifteen, my father decided that he wanted to see how much his little girl had grown and proceeded to slip his hand down into my underwear. I was so angry and disappointed in him. I pulled his hands away telling him, "You don't need to use your hands to see". I couldn't find the words to adequately describe to my mother why I didn't want to spend time with my dad and she always insisted that I go anyway. It was part of a process for my learning that what I felt didn't matter. And then there was my mother's boyfriend who constantly teased me about my breast size and counted the years till I would be old enough to tour his bedroom. He seemed to me to be a creepy kind of guy. Outside appearances showed a guy who was fun, fatherly, ordinary, and caring. I was disgusted by his greasy grins that he would show off when he had gotten out yet another sly trick. My insides rotted when he'd hug me or slobber his wet kisses on me from his yellowed chewing tobacco teeth, and stale pipe smoke or beer breath. He did help my mom a lot financially and with fixing up things around the apartment but I could never get past him running her down all time under the guise of joking around. I cringed to hear him refer to her as a "fat cow", and to see her tune it out as a perfectly acceptable joke.

He was a dirty-minded fellow, too, who took every opportunity to grab a woman's breast. One day he made the mistake of grabbing Dana's breast. He messed with the wrong one. She grabbed him by his arms, and pushed him against the wall warning him to never lay a hand on her again. I think he got the fright of his life, and a little lesson in humility. I tried to be tough with him, being stern with the way he spoke to me or grabbed at me, but it always seemed to fall on deaf ears. Mom wasn't much help because she would make excuses for him and laugh at his digs at me. I never understood how she could be so blind to it. I realize now that she had her own troubles, and her own inner world to escape to as she went through motions of pretending to have a happy life. She wasn't able to hear me even if she wanted to. For many, many years I hated her and blamed her, but not anymore. I learned the peace and overwhelming freedom that is mine once I let go of blame.

My older sister, Dana, again took me under her wing, and at one point wanted to adopt me. We talked about it a great deal. I wanted to agree to it, but it meant a legal process and having to prove why it was not healthy or safe for me to stay with my mother. A phone call from my grandmother made the decision for me. She had told me that if I did that to my own mother, then she could no longer be my grandmother. I was so deeply hurt because I loved my grandma. She fussed over me and made me feel special.

I grew up with the image of her grandmother as the epitome of "mother" with her gentle touch and homemade goodies to nourish us. Her home was like a doll's house, straight out of a magazine, and she was always stylishly dressed in her coordinated outfits. She always seemed to have a way of fixing things, bandaging the wounds, reminding us of what family means. She had raised four daughters and was steadfastly loyal to her husband and children. Hearing her say that she couldn't support me in living with my sister brought up my fears of losing the only sense of what a real family was supposed to look like. Looking at it now, there's a recognition that she was only doing the best she knew how to do in an effort to protect her own daughter. So I stayed with my mother to put up with a few more years of the abuse of mom's boyfriend and feeling invisible, all the while hating my mother and feeling so much shame for it.

I couldn't stand to look at myself in the mirror, and instead looked past myself searching for something more, wanting desperately for there to be more. My world continued to be a lonely, dark cloud of confused emotions. My time was mostly spent alone, lost in sinister thoughts about the cruelty of life and feeling so completely lost in a place where I didn't belong. There were endless hours of dwelling on plans to end my life. I hated my existence, but became convinced that I was being over-dramatic and that there were people out there going through worse than me. I couldn't even take comfort in my own self-pity. It seemed like I carried an anchor around my neck that was slowly drowning me.

One day, while watching a religious program on television I felt that the person on the screen was talking to me, offering the promise of something so wonderful as to cure me of my gloom. I would have given anything at this point to be pulled free from the darkness. Like so many people desperately seeking salvation, I picked up the phone and made the call. I remember crying so hard, asking for direction, and praying to God to bring me a feeling of being loved. Even now, it seems like such a silly thing to have done. I don't remember exactly how old I was then, maybe fifteen or sixteen. It doesn't matter, I guess. What matters is that, however I might have interpreted it, that phone call planted a seed of hope that many years later would confirm that God was with me all along.

There was an almost desperate need to feel good about myself, to feel worth something. School became my lifeline. My teachers had taken me under their wings and I received praises and recognition that was soaked up in some twisted sense of neediness and survival. I developed near obsessive crushes on a couple of my female teachers and developed many delusions about them taking me home, adopting me as their own and moving to place of happy-ever-after. It was worth putting up with the scorn and ridicule felt from my classmates just so I could capture fleeting moments of acceptance which I lapped up like a starving kitten.

I latched on to my mother's youngest sister who had become my safe harbor. I adored her and wanted to always be around her. She always knew exactly what to say to help me feel better. She was another person who seemed to have her life figured out and was so full of strength, determination, gusto, and stylish appearance. She was smart, beautiful, devilishly witty, and so gentle and loving. She was young at heart and had such an appreciation for life. I just loved being in her company, regardless of what we were doing. At times, I wished desperately that she could have been my mother, but maybe it was better just the way it was. Even with her, it was difficult to find the words to accurately explain what was really going on inside. My relationship with my aunt served as a thorn in my mother's side for many years. It sparked a lot of jealousy and insecurity. Thankfully, they were able to move past that to enjoy a more loving and accepting relationship.

Thinking back over the years, I realize that I had latched on to a lot of different people, always hoping that they could bring me to a place of feeling truly loved. It would take going through a lot of embarrassment, rejection, and humiliation before finally coming to realize that the love would have to come from inside myself.

I performed in concerts, gave speeches in competitions, acted in stage plays, and was very good at it. However, as soon as the show was over and I had to step back into my dull life, the depression took over again. I hated for the show to end. At the end of the school day, I would even hang out around school to read or work in the library, just to avoid having to go home to a place that felt so lonely and the air too heavy with sadness. Somewhere along the way, I seemed to stop breathing. There was only enough breath to sustain me in physically being alive. What a sad creature I was.

One consolation for me was having Ginger's company and eventually a gray long-haired tabby. I thought I had lost my cat once when the apartment building had caught fire. We couldn't find the cat anywhere. I cried so hard, feeling for the loneliness that would come without her. I begged and pleaded for her until eventually my next door neighbor went back into the apartment and found her huddled behind the couch, shivering and scared by the sirens of the fire truck. She was handed to me and I huddled with her under my blanket so thankful she was there.

Ginger became an outdoor pet when we moved away from home. I hated having to keep her outside. She had always been a part of the family, sleeping on our bed or sitting close by at all times. I would stand in the window just to talk to her so she wouldn't feel so alone behind the house. When mom wasn't home, I would bring her inside to be with me. She was getting pretty old by now and would often have seizures. It was like she knew what was happening and she'd look up with a certain look in her eyes, as if to offer a warning of what was coming. With a thump, she'd fall to the floor, her paws stiffening in a crook behind her head. It was so frightening to watch and every time, I thought that this might be it for her. I sat beside her, gently stroking her back and talking to her, offering some reassurance. My tears would fall upon her, mixing with the foaming saliva from her mouth. She always came through and then weakly crawled over to sit upon my lap, looking up at me with a look of relief in her eyes. It's like we shared a mutual suffering and offered each other companionship to get through it.

In my emotional suffering, I started to drift into a world of make-believe and created endless fantasies of being carried away by a stunningly beautiful creature. The odd thing about this image was that this creature was always in the form of a woman.

There were daydreams about getting married; settling down with a house, a dog, and a cat, but there was never an image of a husband. I never understood why it didn't fit, but just somehow accepted that one day it would. The whole idea of marriage was too obscure for me to imagine and the idea of bringing children into such turmoil was definitely out of the question.

As much as I dreamed about an ideal, happy life, somehow it never got to the point of really believing in it. Every night brought a disappearance into some other world while the moon and stars comforted me. I continued to dream about anything my imagination would allow in taking me away from my life.

Dreaming With A Friend

April 1987 ~ age 15

Bright, beautiful moon
shining the whole night through,
as I sleep a restless sleep,
let me dream along with you.
Cover my face and pillow
with your magnificent light.
Wash away my tears
and stay with me tonight.
So high above in the sky,
you're like a mountain stream.
Your moonlight cascades over me
delivering a peaceful dream.
I lay in your gentle embrace
thinking of those I love
and thinking of you,
so close yet so high above.

All good things come to an end
and then it's time for us to part.
Tomorrow must always come,
a new day must always start.
When the sun begins to rise
and the daylight hours draw near,
you seek to find your hiding place
and suddenly disappear.
I wait for the night to return
like it always did before
so that we can be together
to share our dreams once more.

If Tomorrow Comes

January 7, 1989 ~ age 16

I have cried a thousand tears
to release my anger and pain.
My pillow has been drowned
by the constant fear of defeat.
I lay in bed every night
staring into the darkness
Wondering about tomorrow
and everything that is to come.
Maybe I am doomed to depression

for the rest of my life.
Fear... that's what it is.
The fear of failing those I love.
Fear that I won't be good enough.
It clutches me in its palms.
Confusion, doubt, and resistance
Surrounds me.
I am confused by the facts.
I am doubtful of my victory.
Yet, I am resistant to defeat.
I have not yet begun to fight
For the real battle hasn't come yet.
I am gathering my weapons,
Knowledge, confidence, and strength.
With these things
May I someday reach my goal
And discover tomorrow.

I don't really know what saved me from that; what kept me going. Maybe it was a number of things. I remember one day in grade seven Cultural Studies class, my teacher had shared a Lao Tzu quote with us. "Give a man a fish and you feed him for a day. Teach a man to fish and you feed him for a lifetime". That sent a chill through me when I heard it because there was such resounding truth in it. I think it was then when I first had a glimpse of recognition of something far greater than the miserable world I found myself surrounded by. Now when I repeat those words, it reverberates deep in my soul as a reminder of how each one of us is a Master, holding the capacity to affect the world by a simple gesture.

A mentor in High School, my homeroom teacher, served a pivotal role in my believing in myself. In many ways, he was a father figure to me. He was a gentle, soft-spoken man, with a very non-assuming presence. He was very patient and showed genuine concern for his students. When he looked at me, he really absorbed what I had to say and for once I didn't feel invisible. He inspired me with many thought provoking conversations about seeing beyond the obvious. We once debated about what the world might be if only everyone just supported each other instead of competing, that we could all use our abilities to mutually support each other. It's pretty amazing to me now, to realize I was thinking that way at 17 years old.

Chapter Three
Pandora's Box

Release from high school hell couldn't come fast enough and I was eager to set out into the broader world that I dreamed of. Once I went on to university, life gradually started to change. It was good to get away from the unhappy home and away from my mother. I had been doing some kind of dance with her, in a feeling of loving her and hating her at the same time, blaming her for not being what I needed her to be, for not protecting me, and most of all for not hearing me. One time I had written her a very angry letter, vowing to be her daughter in name only. I remember listening from my bedroom as mother cried her tears over that letter, and felt my heart rip. How could I have been so cruel? I tried to make up for it but don't know if it could ever have been undone. As much as I wanted to be able to love her, I was too consumed in my own self-pity.

My university life started to offer me a way of breaking free. Meeting new people, enrolling in philosophy and science and language courses, and having some independence gave me the opportunity to start observing more closely the intricate workings of my life. One day while searching through the library book stacks, one book in particular stole my attention. *Seth Speaks* , a channeled text offered through Jane Roberts, was unlike any book I had ever read before and strangely enough, it seemed to offer me answers that I didn't know I had been looking for. I questioned my beliefs, my values, and my place in the world. Somehow sparks of light still shone through the darkness. Some deep seed of truth still grew inside of me. Perhaps that little girl still danced in the woods with the fairies.

The light of Love

April 27, 1992 ~ age 20

Much can be seen
in a beautiful rose,
the epitome of perfection,
beauty, and grace.
In the sunshine
there is happiness and joy
and a warmth that reaches
the depths of your soul.
In the rain and in tears
there is passion.
sometimes violent and strong,
sometimes soft and subtle.
In the midst of winter
there is hope
as new life waits
to be set free.
In everything
there is goodness.
In everything
there is the light of love.

I met my first romantic partner soon after going to university. Up to this point, I still had no real idea of romance, let alone with a woman. I had gone on a few dates with boys, even had a boyfriend in high school, but couldn't stand being around him. Dating Brad was part of a requirement to be like everyone else. He was an average kind of guy, not too bad looking, but not overly bright. He wasn't popular and often cracked jokes that really weren't funny at all. He was very insecure and came across as pretty goofy at times. He tried to be a cool dude but it seemed that the harder he tried, the goofier he was. I felt sorry for him, even sorrier that for having gotten mixed up with him at all. Still, everyone was so pleased to finally see me with a boyfriend. Perhaps it was more reassuring to them than it was for me.

At my 16th birthday party, the whole gang gathered around and put us on the spot, teasing me with the line "sweet sixteen and never been kissed". It was awful. I hated having to kiss him, but that was what supposed to happen to be like everyone else. It was awkward, forced, and I almost had to hold my breath to get through it because my insides were churning. Brad started to plan out our life together, how we would get married and I would stay home to have his babies and cook his meals. I burst that bubble pretty quick, telling him with certainty that I was not going to be someone's domestic slave. I had a life of my own to live and had no intention of staying with him.

What really turned me from Brad was his pushiness to be closer when I clearly told him no. I distinctly remember one day he had driven into town to see me. He brought his best friend with him. The three of us were sitting in my living room and Brad wanted to lay down on the couch with me. Pretty dumb idea considering his best friend was sitting right there. He tried to force me to lie down in spite of my protests and the insistence of his friend to leave me alone. I kicked him out of the house and told him to never come back unless he could treat me with more respect. It didn't take me very long to put an end to that charade of a relationship.

I made one other attempt to be in a so-called normal relationship with a guy. I met up with Mitch shortly after starting University. We had been friends for a while, since he was Brad's best friend. We had spent many hours talking and sharing our thoughts. He was taller than me, with fair-hair and bluish green eyes. He always had such a fresh, natural appearance and a softness and gentleness in the way he spoke. He was sensitive and deep and so compassionate. We shared our love of music, fine arts, and the theatre. We talked about philosophy and life. It only took one date to realize how wrong it felt. I couldn't stand the idea of any guy touching me in the way a man and woman are supposed to touch, not even this beautiful soul. For a while I tried to hold on desperately to the idea of having a normal life and tried to convince myself that I loved him enough to eventually get past my reservations, but I just couldn't. He left for the mainland and I wouldn't see him again for almost two years later, when he made another attempt to contact me. I didn't have the courage to tell him the truth; that I really broke up with him because I was falling in love with a woman.

The relationship that developed with Rochelle was so beautifully coordinated in a love story that could easily be construed as a fairy tale, just like the ones that were created in my childhood dreams. It unfolded so naturally and comfortably that I knew in my heart it was right. We had met in the first few days of starting college. We would keep running into each other in the hall and there seemed to be a level of ease between us, just like friends who had known each other for years. We eventually started planning our meetings and as friends do, we talked about everything imaginable. Our conversations grew very deep and meaningful as we shared intimate details of our lives and expanded our awareness of the vast universe. Rochelle was the first person I had ever spoken to who seemed to see things the way I did.

As the weeks and months passed by, we found that we wanted to be spending more and more time together. We were there for each other to encourage, to motivate, to inspire, to create, to dream, and also to be purely silly and crazy with. We ran through rain puddles together and danced through the snow like children, walked each other to our classes, stood in the park on cold winter mornings to watch the sun rise together, and held each other when tears came.

One day I was with Rochelle when I received news that Ginger had died. Ginger had been left with my sister Rebecca since mom wasn't able to keep her in the apartment building she moved into in St. John's. Our beloved family pet was reduced to being housed in a pen behind the house because Rebecca's husband wouldn't allow her to be in the house. One brutally cold winter's night this beautiful and fragile little creature was subjected to a night of slowly slipping away to her death. I was devastated and couldn't bear the thoughts of how she suffered, left all alone. After fourteen years with us, she deserved so much better. I grieved for her for a very long time. Rochelle honored my grief and even assisted me in a memorial of sorts to honor her spirit.

My friendship with Rochelle was deepening in a way that neither of us could really name, but we both recognized the warmth, safety, and comfortableness we felt when we were together. She told me one day that I had opened a pandora's box in her. I didn't really know what she had meant but didn't question it. When we first kissed, I knew inside how perfect it was for us. It was a far cry from the awkward and messy kisses from my first boyfriend. Rochelle awakened a side of me that allowed me to truly feel desirable and worthy. She was a rare gift, a real blessing and she remains in my heart even now.

After two years together, Rochelle grew restless in her new found identity and started to feel it was time for her to move on. I resisted this, of course, and didn't make it easy for her. It looked like the impossible to ever find anyone that would feel so right for me like she had been. The end of that relationship started me on an entirely different journey. I tried to find a sense of self in the middle of a controversial lifestyle filled with heartbreak, disorder, confusion, instability, and games.

The initial footloose days of finally feeling like a part of something was great. I enjoyed the fleeting moments of camaraderie among my own kind. Then I went head long into years of playing a role, at every moment trying to ensure being loved and wanted. The string of relationships that followed was an allowance of being used despite my insides telling me how wrong it was. It felt like a hollow shell of existence. Still, I managed to catch the fleeting glimpses of sunlight reflecting off the dampened trees or the beads of water sitting in the folds of blooming flowers, and thinking about this whole other world that possibly existed and where I wanted to escape.

Identity

April 10, 1992 ~ age 20

Who am I?

I have dreams of a world at peace

and a world where everyone is my friend.

Who am I,

with my face just one in many

of thousands like me, yet individual from me?

The blood in my veins is the same as theirs,

those countless faces that turn their backs to me.

I am a symbol of all they want to be

but they are too afraid to be different

from the entirety.

I am the hope of all those with no hope

for a future of peace within ourselves.

Why?

June 9, 1992 ~ age 20

Why the suffering and the pain?

Why the continuous struggle?

We are only teased with the rays of sun

when the dark clouds once again set in.

Is this a test of wills? Of courage? Of strength?

Is there really good in evil,

or is there evil behind the good?

Why must we live if we only have to die?

Why do we bother to try,

when we only have to live it again?

My life was being slowly sucked down a drain. I started acting out in all kinds of ways and got involved in relationships that depleted my energy and motivation to improve myself. The dynamics at play in my life triggered my old, unhealthy ways of coping. It was quite a messed up existence and again I felt like I was drowning. I soon grew very tired of the partying and the shallow layers of identification that came with this life. God knows, I made my mistakes and did some really crazy things. Maybe it was in doing those things that I finally started to see the truth.

The Tides of Life

May 20, 1993 ~ age 21

How do I explain the feelings I have?

A darkness setting in, a coldness deep inside?

The hurt and the pain creeps up

and then suddenly it goes away again.

How do I explain the changes I go through?

The sadness, the anger, the love, the joy?
It never remains constant, always changing.
It shifts like the sands of time, like the tides of the sea.
How will I know when the healing has worked,
when I will no longer feel out of control?
So many questions, so much confusion.
I feel lost and drifting in a sea of uncertainty.

My Dear Child

March 11, 1994 ~ age 22

I sit here wondering, thinking, questioning,
where have I come from? Where am I going?
I try to look within to find the child
that I lost so long ago;
my inner child who never grew up
who never got past the pain.
Why is she so afraid?
Why does she feel so alone?
Perhaps she never learned
to look past the tears.
Perhaps she isn't seeing
the strong woman she has become.

One night as I lay in bed starting to drift into sleep, something happened that I still cannot fully comprehend. I've heard of such things as hag dreams, maybe this was one of them. My body slowly went paralyzed as a wave of cool, tingly sensations moved from my feet along my whole body, up to the top of my head. My head fell to one side and left me utterly helpless to do anything. I had enough awareness to know that it wasn't a dream. My mind raced with questions about what was happening to me. Through the darkness I heard a quiet voice calling to me. It was a child's voice, sounding scared. It kept saying, "Help me". I tried to ask who she was, what I could do, but the paralysis prevented me from doing anything except breathing. Mentally I relayed my thoughts to say, "I hear you. I want to help. Please tell me what to do". With that, the voice disappeared and that cool wave once again washed back down across my body, releasing me from the paralysis state. As strange as that experience was for me, I locked it away and never shared it because it seemed to just confirm how crazy my life was.

At one point, the military offered hopes of providing the kind of structure my life needed. All the tests were passed with ease and before long I was geared up in my snazzy uniform and marching in tune with the drills. It was exciting to have a spiffy uniform to wear and to feel a part of something really important. Very early into the game though, I realized what kind of price would have to be paid for the privilege of wearing that uniform. It's true what they say about the military taking away your identity. From day one, the role being played was strikingly obvious. A couple of girls quickly swooped in on me, seeming to pick up on the unspoken recognition of one of their own kind. But I knew I could never live my life under pretense and play a role according to what some system of rules determined. The military days were very short lived and the ticket out of there was to use my history of depression as the excuse for bailing out. It's crossed my mind now and again, wondering where I would be now if I had stayed. Maybe I would have a decorated uniform and many tales of exciting travels. Then again, I have my exciting tales now without the military.

For a period of time a diet of anti-depressant medications and regular visits to the psychiatrist kept me going. It wouldn't be the first time. When I first started university, a counselor was helping me to let go of some of the self-blame, but the deeper work was a little too scary at the time. The first psychiatrist I went to see immediately targeted my sexuality as the source of all my difficulties and he quickly jumped on writing me a prescription of the drug that would cure me. That could have been disastrous had I not been strong enough in my sense of self. He really wasn't hearing me. It was one of the clearest examples of listening to my own inner voice and acting on recognition of what wasn't right. I promptly cleared up that fiasco.

I was about to give up on the whole idea of counseling when I finally met a Psychiatrist who truly seemed tuned in. He really heard me, and he seemed to have a genuine caring and respect for who I was as a soul. He saw beyond the layers of presentation. He spoke to me as a human being, not as a Doctor to a patient. He asked about my inner beliefs and feelings, not about the reactionary behaviors of the chaos around me. I truly felt heard and appreciated his willingness to value my own insights.

The Shift

August 5, 1996 ~ age 24

The ever-changing tides of time
drifting from today into tomorrow,
ever-growing, ever-reaching
trying to hold on to some semblance
of a past faded and worn;
grasping onto the glitter of a future,
however uncertain,
promising something better
than what's left behind.

Separate Worlds

February 10, 1997 ~ age 25

From the outside
the joyous sounds of happiness
filter through the walls
and dance upon the ears
like the drumming of raindrops
upon an empty bucket.
From the outside
only traces of warmth are felt

radiating from the hearth,
painfully drawing nearer to coldness;
creeping to frozen interior.
Looking in,
the splendor of comfort,
of inviting eyes, enchanting smiles,
beacon to the hollow coves
of long forgotten memories.
Looking in
through the fragile panes
which separate worlds
becomes frosted with the contact
of coldness upon inner warmth.
Scraping through the frost
desperately seeking a glimpse,
a slight sensation of happiness,
becomes a struggle
to one who is
isolated, abandoned, alone,
always left
on the outside, looking in.

Chapter Four
An Empty Dream

I went through a long stretch of time of completely tuning out, barely finding the focus or motivation to follow through on my studies. I lived for the weekend, for another chance to step into my role and hopefully find that special someone who would help me turn my life around. It wasn't difficult to find someone willing to step in and play the game. We stumbled upon one another at the infamous bar where all lonely souls go with eternal optimism of finding love. We were two gloomy souls carrying a great deal of disillusionment about life. We had no real desire or intention to become involved but we seemed to cling on to one another and offer some comfort while we wallowed in our misery.

Shelby was significantly older than me, but emotionally quite young. She had a fairy-like quality about her that really appealed to me. She was fun-loving, playful, and in many ways innocent and naive. With her slight frame and fair skin, I could easily see her dancing in the woods with the fairies. Maybe I was trying to retrieve some of that magic I had lost so long ago. Our stumbling upon one another immediately put me in a role of caretaker. That same night, Shelby was so drunk and chilled that she could barely find her footing to get herself home, so I went with her. This brought me into another two years of playing a role in a classic co-dependent relationship.

It was during this time, that I really felt that life was spinning out of control. Shelby and I seemed to get into some sort of passive-aggressive type of manipulative game with one another. We were both unemployed, living on assistance, on medications for depression, and getting caught up in the games. I became enmeshed in Shelby's world and completely shut out of my own life. This little fairy had a lot of anger in her and mirrored the shadows that had been clouding me. No matter how hard I tried to be loving and compassionate, it was sucking me deeper into a hole that didn't promise any way out. Again and again, my own needs were put second. At some point the recognition came that I couldn't do this to myself anymore. I needed to get out of it.

In the midst of playing our games, we landed into trouble with the law because of some shoplifting. It's actually hilarious now to think that I was bold enough to fill up a shopping cart and march out the front door. It really had turned into a game. We had gone through the store, taking things out of packages to try it out before tossing it into our cart. Somewhere inside I knew that this is what it was going to take to change things so I played the game to the fullest.

I remember feeling so completely helpless, frustrated, and fed up with my life. It was a loud and clear cry for help, a cry from somewhere deep inside screaming "get me out of here". It was just serious enough to cause me to take a good hard look at what I was doing with my life. Feeling handcuffs about my wrists, having my fingerprints taken, and sitting in a cold, dark cell with a bare stained mattress while the girls in the next cell taunted and teased was a deeply humbling experience. It truly shocked me into the realization of how I had become so passive in allowing my life to go down the tubes.

Once again, my guardian angels assisted me by casting light into my vision to help me find my way. On some deep inner level, I had asked the right questions to find a better way. It wouldn't be until many years later that I would get to know these angels on a more personal level, but I can say in all certainty now that it was they who helped lift me out of my despair. Somehow my angels, and the support of my psychiatrist, offered me an easier road to pay my penance instead of being sent to jail for the six month term the courts had been considering. I served out my time in a community agency where I could exercise independence and freedom. In the end, I was deeply grateful for the experience because it diverted me towards the higher road.

A decision was made to change the direction of my life. I refused to allow myself to get sucked any further down this spiral of destruction that had already started. Some shift happened inside and seeds of deeper meaning were planted. As I started to make more loving decisions and recognize my worth, it opened the door to an honest to goodness real partner. Up to this point, the whole idea of relationships had become a distant dream and there seemed to be no hope left of ever meeting anyone who was normal.

A mutual friend made the connection between Ana and myself. I was pinching myself with disbelief. Ana was a single mom, professional, and had never been in a real relationship before. I admired her dedication to raising her daughter while putting herself through college and starting a career. She was a woman of substance, not like the women I had been meeting previously. She was smart, genuine, deep, and naturally beautiful, with the most amazing smile I had ever seen. When she laughed, her eyes sparkled and she glowed with life. She didn't pretend and didn't put on some big courting ritual to grab my attention. She was real. It scared me, both because I had never had it before and because I was afraid of losing it once she knew what my life was about. We would spend the next eight years together. For many reasons, it would have made sense to start my story here, because this is where I really started to wake up.

After years of being involved in less than desirable relationships, and drifting through my life with no real sense of direction or purpose, I finally met a woman who seemed to want the same things I did. There was nothing very traditional about our relationship, yet everything about it was so traditional. We met. We fell in love. We moved in together. Ana supported me in graduating from University with my degree and starting my career as a Counsellor in a Residential Center. We started cooking meals, keeping house, and tending to our garden. Even her daughter accepted me into their life, at least after a time of the testing and figuring out just how I fit into the picture.

Casey was a typical, scrawny nine year old girl, full of ideas for adventures and experiments. She adored her mother and always wanted to have a part in the projects her mother worked on. Casey was a bright, creative, energetic, compassionate, and inventive little girl who would over the next few years challenge me in endless ways to stretch beyond my comfort zone. She had a number of friends but didn't consider herself to be very popular. She preferred to hang out with her friends away from the house, because she wasn't quite ready yet to let them know about her two moms. She never quite reached a place of full acceptance of me as a parent, but in her own way, she made room for me in her life.

Over the years, we shared in the joys and in the tears. We had many disagreements, but somehow we seemed to have this understanding between us to not take things too personally. It frazzled me sometimes to see Casey brush it off with such nonchalance. Ana would often get upset at us for arguing but we would remind her that we were simply disagreeing and in a little while it would be back to normal. Still, I was never quite completely included in the loop to truly be a parent to Casey. The final decisions and plans and disciplines rested on Ana's shoulders.

We became a family. We seemed to have a perfectly normal, common, every-day type of life. I had an opportunity to learn a little about being a parent, along with the good and the bad. We made plans for our life together. It was a beautiful time. It was the closest I had ever come to having everything I dreamed of having. Even now, I can look back and feel warmth and joy in my heart for the blessings it brought into my life, even with the challenges.

Our families accepted us and embraced our life together, which was a novelty for me because prior to this, even though my family knew about my life, they never quite managed to fully embrace it. Even my mother, who previously had been detached towards my girlfriends, had seemed to reach a place of acceptance. Ana's mother became a special person to me. It touched my heart to feel her acceptance. I remember one day she was visiting. Ana and I were having some little disagreement over something our cat was doing. Ana's mother spoke up and chuckled. She pointed out that if all we had to disagree about was a stupid little cat, then we ought to count our blessings. She was right. Up to that point, we never fought. We co-existed in a beautiful flow of acceptance and support. It was a nice little reminder of how blessed I felt.

We made plans to have a child together; something I had never dreamed would happen but it somehow now seemed to make perfect sense. I suddenly felt such a deep yearning to mother a child. I remember once when my older sister was pregnant that I had told her with absolute conviction that I would never have children. She proceeded to describe to me the awesome feeling of carrying a child and the stirrings inside. Now I was starting to understand how that might feel. I went through the process of meeting with a Fertility Specialist and opened the door to my new journey. I was so excited about my chance to be a mother and felt so deeply grateful for the new life that Ana was giving me. I'm not really sure why but when I shared the exciting news with Ana, she closed that door again. At the time, it was devastating to me and I was not prepared to go the journey alone so I let it go. Now I can look back and feel that Ana did me a great service by not allowing me to go down that road because it would have been for the wrong reasons. Motherhood promised the blessing of having someone to truly love me and depend on me. It would have been a twisted ego version of how love is extended.

As the years blended together my relationship with Ana began to fade into an uncomfortable acceptance. It became a rehearsed routine, lacking in any real enjoyment. We experienced many changes and challenges together, including the death of Ana's mother, the reconnection with her estranged father, and the disagreements on the parenting responsibilities of Ana's daughter. There was a widening gulf between us. I think we both went into a place of merely bobbing along without having the heart to really put a voice to the distance that had come between us. I truly didn't want to face the prospect of the single scene again. I had experienced all I wanted or needed to experience of that scene, filled with its dramas and head games. I was content to stay where I was, thinking that this is a good as it's going to get. It really wasn't so bad. We carried through on the expected rituals of what partners do. We bought a house together and tried to develop some semblance of a stable, happy life. It didn't work. It drove us further apart and this unsettledness spilled over into my career, or maybe my unhappiness spilled over into my relationship. Either way, I felt the deepening sense of discontentment. Thank goodness that I hadn't brought a child into this.

The real acknowledgement of the distance between us came to me one day at Cape Spear. Ana and I were watching as a huge iceberg turning over in the water, with chunks of it crumbling away. As I breathed in the energy of that shift, somewhere deep inside I recognized the symbolism of it. My relationship was crumbling and falling away, twisting and churning painfully as we stubbornly clung to something that was no longer loving. It was uncovering the hidden depths of myself. I looked at Ana and felt a chill in my heart. I knew that it was the beginning of the end for us. She was right there beside me, witnessing with me this spectacular event that I might never behold again. Yet, I never felt more removed or distant from her. I turned away because it was too hard to bear. I wasn't ready to admit to it, but Ana was lost to me.

At this very moment, there was someone witnessing the very same scene. I didn't know it at the time, but this someone would soon come into my life in a very significant way. I felt compelled to look across the parking lot and my eyes fell upon someone running to their car to get a camera. I watched, feeling a pull that I couldn't explain. I wanted to go over to them and talk to them. Somewhere inside me I felt that it was showing me a glimpse of a whole new life waiting for me.

Not long after that, I was given a book that changed everything. It seems quite ironic now that it was a gift from Ana. Is it possible that her soul knew that her showing up in my life was to push me into waking up to who I truly was? Dr. Phil McGrath's *Self Matters* introduced me to my authentic self. Suddenly my world as I knew it started crashing down and for the first time since lying in the beds of ferns with my fairy friends, I was able to allow myself to fully breathe. For all the times I drove my car to the edge of the cliffs to watch the crashing waves below and wondered about the prospect of diving into those waves, this discovery of uncovering my authentic self offered a ray of hope. I started reading other books of spiritual insights; although at the time I didn't fully grasp the depth of the spiritual journey I was undertaking. *The Celestine Prophesy*, among others sat on my bookshelf, seeming to call to me. I occasionally picked it up and read tiny portions. It would be a year later before I was truly ready for it. I could no longer hide from what was permeating through my heart as a warning to pay attention to my slow, painful, suffocating existence. I made a conscious choice to start truly paying attention to what was in my heart.

One day I was sitting in front of the computer working on some mundane project. Ana had come downstairs and she took some interest in my work. She had started to walk away to go back upstairs, but then she hesitated. She turned around to look at me and said something like "you know, you're really something. You are really good at what you do. I just thought I would tell you that". I don't recall the exact words, but the energy of that moment was like a lightening bolt. It was the first time in a very long time that I felt she actually could see me. She actually recognized me. I wasn't invisible after all. It saddened me to think that all these years had gone by, and we hadn't taken notice enough to honour one another's presence. Did this come too late, or was the recognition shining through at just the right time to embrace the truth that waited for me?

I decided one day that I had enough and told Ana that this was it for me. It was such a painful experience. I still loved her so very much and still wanted for our life to be what I thought it was supposed to be. As she lay in my arms that night and cried, I felt my heart tearing apart. There was a glimpse of such a deep and abiding love, something that I had wanted to see for a long time but believed it wasn't there. My guilt set in and out of a sense of duty, I made the decision to stay. I knew immediately that it was not the right decision because I felt the dark cloud envelop me again and suddenly the new found breath had been squeezed out of me. We stayed together a while longer to continue playing out our drama. Months later, something also shifted in her and we reached the final breaking point. It truly was over. Sadly, we chose to allow it to unfold in much anger and cruelty. For whatever reason, that is how we needed to let it go. How utterly foolish we humans can be in allowing something so beautiful to disintegrate into such ugliness.

For a number of weeks following, the drama continued to unfold as we were bound to one another through legalities of home ownership. At times we were civil. At times we were nasty. One day, I recognized that my freedom was more important than trying to hold unto this charade. Asking myself some very difficult questions, I was forced to admit that I was trying to hold on to something that was nothing more than an illusion and that this would never bring me happiness. I walked away from it all. All the dreams that once seemed so valuable suddenly meant nothing. It was causing me to smother in a swirling cloud of emotions. I had to let go in order to finally understand the stability that was waiting for me in Spirit.

That was the first real choice I had ever made to love myself enough. It was the beginning of a long road of opportunities to exercise my faith and my courage. I was beginning on a road where I truly had to start fresh with establishing new friendships, new social circles, and live on my own for really the first time in my life. Funnily enough, it was also the beginning of a sort of friendship with Casey, the now adult daughter that I helped raise.

As she stood in my doorway getting ready to leave after a visit, Casey vindicated me. She told me that she finally understood my attempts to be a mother to her and to help offer her guidance and structure. In an odd sort of way, she released me from the guilt I had been feeling for having failed her. In that moment, I truly appreciated her brilliance and the perfection of our shared experiences. We emerged as friends.

I really had only one friend at this time and relied on him a great deal. I don't know where I would have been without Daniel's support and patience. We had met a couple of years prior to this, having been employed in the same organization. Daniel was a tall, lean, handsome man with a beautiful presence that immediately offered a sense of comfortableness and acceptance. I was too caught up in my own miserable existence to allow a friendship to develop and had become quite expert at keeping people out while isolating myself from any semblance of a social life. But Daniel and I seemed to connect. We had somehow identified a soul connection to one another, although we didn't verbalize this at the time. We seemed to have found a way to interact in our work and support each other's ideas in a way that our colleagues didn't quite get. Daniel soon moved on to another place and despite his attempt to keep the connection, I hadn't allowed it.

One day as I was sitting at home reflecting on how shallow my life had become and then thought about this man who had tried so many times to befriend me. On a whim I called him up and suggested we get together for coffee. That phone call engaged one of the truest friendships I have ever known. It was the first time of truly allowing any man to come into the intimate circle of my life and into my trust. The full significance of this friendship wouldn't be fully realized for quite some time later.

Chapter Five

Soul Encounter

Nurturing wounds over lost love and feeling completely drained of enthusiasm for anything in life, I decided to sign up for a retreat to be immersed in the company of other women from all walks of life and all modalities of healing. At the time, Ana had suggested that we go together as an attempt to do some repair on our relationship. I responded with conviction that this was for me alone because the next leg of the journey would be for my own healing. This retreat offered glimpses of the depths of human caring, compassion, and genuine friendship. This was my time to unwind and start to do some true soul searching into what I wanted my life to look like. I heard so many stories of healing and inspiration that my soul truly started to breathe for the first time. A whole new existence opened up to me and I felt a renewed sense of enthusiasm for life and all its possibilities. It was a chance to start everything new, an opening to acknowledge many aspects of myself that I had long forgotten about. It was an illumination of the thread of Spirit that had weaved its way through my existence and supported me through it all.

Here, at this gathering, I received some vindication that I wasn't crazy. It was here where I would meet one of my greatest teachers; one that would trigger a whirlwind of growth in my spirit and leave an impression in my heart that would sustain me through my difficult trials. The synchronistic events were unfolding because that mysterious stranger I had seen at the crashing iceberg was now right here. The realization that she was the person from the iceberg scene wouldn't come to me until much later as I started to get to know her.

I had heard about the idea of having encounters with soul mates, individuals who for some unknown reason seem extremely familiar and this strikes a chord of resonance deep inside of you. When it happened to me for the first time, it sent me into a state of near panic. The powerful feelings and energy that moved through me upon seeing this radiant presence was more than could be digested.

A room full of people were gathering and I took a seat to wait for everyone to settle into their place. On the other side of the room, some people were making their way into the room from the hallway. Behind this group of people, I caught a glimpse of a woman that I had never seen before. It was as if I'd been struck by lightening. She seemed to literally glow. There was a light emanating from around her making it seem like she was an apparition. I was torn between a sense of joyfulness and a kind of unsettling fear. For some reason I could not in any way explain, I had a strong recognition and acceptance that this person is, and would be, very important in my life. The static electricity that flowed through this moment told me with certainty that this woman held a key for me. This image of her would be burned into my memory to haunt me.

I watched her for a little while; mesmerized by the way she seemed to float through the room. She had a dazzling smile and when she stopped to speak with people, she had a sweet and gentle way of lightly touching them. Images flashed through my mind of something I couldn't possibly describe. How could I feel so connected to her and feel this familiarity when I only just saw her for the first time? I didn't even know her name. Later she would be introduced as Kathleen. At the time, I pushed aside these confusing feelings, having no way of referencing what it all meant. As much as I kept pushing it aside, it kept coming back. For months afterwards, and even now, the energy of that first encounter still sent shivers through me.

Perhaps a month had passed since our first meeting, and I bumped into Kathleen again. We shared a little conversation. It was all very casual and friendly, but it was enough to show me a glimpse of the warmth and loveliness of this woman. A little foolishly perhaps, I wrote her a letter. I didn't really understand it at the time, and hadn't come to that place yet of recognizing who she really was to me, but I felt compelled to write to her, thanking her for sharing a moment with me. As soon as I felt the letter slip from my fingers into the mail box, a magical-like energy swept through me. It was that same electric energy that has swept through me when I had first seen her. It reminded me of the movie *Serendipity* where the winds were swirling about, indicating that the universe was working to bring two people together. I felt a presence come alive in me and felt a sweeping energy in every fibre of my soul and every cell in my body. My insides did somersaults for the joy of this amazing connection I felt. I tried desperately to contain it, but it seemed much more powerful than me.

Over the next several months, I did get opportunities to know Kathleen a little more, and became more deeply drawn into my attraction for her. Unexplainable things started happening, things that seemed to be too much of a coincidence. It was really starting to freak me out. I remember one day sitting on a couch and Kathleen had come over to sit beside me and we chatted. She turned to face me to ask something and for a very brief instant our eyes had met. My body felt as if it had received a jolt and I literally, physically felt as though my body and soul had taken a major leap through space and time to fall deeply into her eyes. It was only for a split second but the shock of it frightened me. I thought maybe she had experienced it too because she nervously looked away. This became yet another image and experience that would burn in me.

The more I started to get to know Kathleen, the more my attraction for her deepened. I saw her sassiness, her joyfulness, her compassion, her gentleness, and her way of encouraging others. I came to love the quirky little things about her, the things that made her human. Kathleen was genuine, the real deal. Her mere presence added a sparkle to the room. She was a vibrant, alluring, mysterious woman. As much as I tried to not be falling for her, I couldn't keep fighting against it. An energetic tide had swept me up and completely consumed me.

My life turned into quite a tumultuous journey after that. My heart and mind became filled with so much confusion, excitement, joy, curiosity, heartache, anger, frustration and utter despair. It brought up all my deepest fears of having to prove myself, fears of being rejected, and it also brought up such strong yearnings to be loved and appreciated. This connection that I was feeling for a woman who was unavailable to me was becoming unbearable. This attraction defied all my logic and went against everything I had always believed in. My heartache and turmoil over Kathleen spilled over into all aspects of my life, causing me to dig deeper and deeper into my own beliefs and desires. It led me to uncover some of the deepest recesses of my shadowed and weakened self. It also illuminated my strengths. It became an amazingly intricate time of healing and purifying.

At the same time, I started having mind-blowing experiences in meditations and dreams. A portal to my childhood magical kingdom was opened. There were numerous times I left my body and traveled with other light beings to be shown the reality that exists beyond what my human mind could imagine. On more than one occasion, I went into my light body and met up with Kathleen. She always seemed to be there despite my efforts against it. Many times, her light body had come to me to hold my hand and to reassure me that on some higher level, all was in perfect order. At times, we held each other's hands and danced in a feeling of pure joy, just as two very dear friends who were reunited. The most powerful moment in that etheric realm happened when her light body had stepped into mine. It was like watching a slow motion film of ghostly images gliding toward one another ever so gracefully and beautifully. Our hands reached out to one another and we drew each other in to hug and hold our hearts together, but then our hearts started beating together in harmony and then magically melded together so that our hearts became one and beat together as one heart. The overwhelming sense of peace, love, and acceptance brought me to tears. It was a true vindication of what I had already known; that on a soul level, we are all one and that it wasn't something to fear but to embrace.

As these experiences came to me, it really caused me a lot of confusion and made it extremely difficult to separate the real from the unreal. I found myself questioning every glance, every gesture, and making assumptions about what all this might really mean. I consulted with card readers and became really messed up with the so-called predictions of how things were unfolding. It challenged my disciplined mind and my values. How could something so pure and so beautiful in the realm of light look so different in the physical realm of human existence?

I started to piece things together and gain a greater understanding of the way human fears operate. As difficult as it was, I faced my own obsessions and delusions in order to come to a place of truth. Kathleen's presence and guidance helped me to see that we have a great responsibility to use our discernment wisely and carefully. Looking back on it now, I can own it and love it as part of the necessary process of coming into my true self. I could not have done it without her. I suppose a sacred contract was honoured. We had come together as two souls agreeing to mirror the very fears we didn't want to face, but had to face in order to evolve in our spirit. I am deeply honoured to have shared that dance with her.

Beginning to explore deeper into this spiritual life, I indulged in every opportunity to participate in workshops and training. I tapped into a long forgotten memory of some essence of myself that had been buried deep inside. A distant echo was drawing nearer, welcoming me home to a place of belonging. All the old feelings of being alone, lost, rejected, and so different from everyone, started to fall away from me like hollow shreds of a long forgotten memory. So long ago, I had made the habit of daily staring into a mirror searching for and hoping for something more, asking what it was all for. Now I was starting to understand. This was hugely significant to me, not only as I tried to resolve the feelings of love in my heart, but also because of the pull towards a greater purpose. It led me to challenge not only my personal relationships but it also brought up many concerns about my career.

My career as a residential counsellor started at the beginning of my relationship with Ana. It seemed significant that both my relationship and my career were dwindling at the same time. I had great appreciation for those I worked with and wanted so much to honour my place with them. A whole chapter of my life was invested in my work assisting individuals with issues of addictions, abuse, mental health concerns, and many other life issues. Perhaps the parallel between my relationship and my career served as a stepping stone in my path of lessons. I was helping my clients sort through their own illusions just as I was sorting through mine. It was here where some of my most profound growth occurred. They all served as my teachers and offered me such valuable insight into the integrity and strength of the human spirit. It was a place that forced you to be real, because if you weren't real, they would sense it a mile away. As I was fumbling through my own trials of relationship break-ups, broken dreams, shattered illusions, and birthing into Spirit, my colleagues and clients offered me daily doses of laughter, love, compassion, and acceptance. Through them I faced many mirrors of my own spirit and grew to love what I was seeing.

A part of me always believed that I would live out my career here, maybe because it had become a comfort zone. Still, I could not ignore the nagging feeling in my heart. There was a long struggle of trying to maintain the enthusiasm for my work; following the routines and taking all the expected steps in building a career. I soon began to realize that this place no longer offered me what was needed to nurture my spirit or support my expansion into the universe. At the end of the day, in spite of efforts to accommodate my new awareness into my work, there was a reverberating call in my heart that grew stronger with each passing day.

The ocean became my best friend throughout this process of sorting through the sordid details of my life. On a daily basis the beach would welcome me and had reserved a place for me to sit with my thermos of coffee, my blanket, and my notebook. It was one place where I could feel free. Hours would pass in meditation, breathing it in and allowing myself the time to laugh or to cry. Sometimes I would even stretch out on the grass and lay back watching the clouds float by, feeling good about being there alone with Spirit. Sometimes it felt very lonely with my heart feeling as though it were breaking apart. The words of Pema Chodron offered comfort to me as she spoke of the experience of a broken heart serving as a breaking open to allow all the love of the universe to flow in. These words became a sort of guidepost for me through my healing journey.

Misplaced destiny

July 7, 2003 ~ age 31

My beating heart
Like thunderous drums
Calls out to you.
Crying echoes in my ears.
The breeze carries your name.
Another place, another time perhaps,
Yet I am here in this time, this place,
Longing for you.

So I sat there on my beach breathing it all in; all the wonders of creation. My broken heart was nurtured as questions were sorted out about why I had to feel such overwhelming love for someone that couldn't be expressed. It became an exploration into the deep recesses of my heart, trying to understand being so drawn into something that couldn't be explained. I thought I would literally crack up from the pressure of being torn in so many directions. Then one day, I felt some energy shift through me. It settled over me like a warm blanket while seemingly releasing all the constrictions that had been bound around my heart. It can only be described as a moment of clarity. Finding my pen, the words flowed onto my paper. For weeks I went into a deeply reflective and profoundly insightful state. Forgiveness came into my heart; forgiveness for myself, for my mother, for my father, and for all being.

August 25, 2003. We set out on this journey trying to find ourselves, to find peace, to find love. We forget to look inside ourselves. Instead we seek refuge in others, sometimes getting caught up in their pain. We so often fail to recognize that what we are seeking is not lost. It is there, always has been there, inside ourselves. The universe is not so vast when we consider that it lies right here within our hearts. We gaze out upon the oceans and the skies, looking for what might lie beyond, wishing, dreaming and hoping to find wondrous treasures beyond the horizon. Stop. Look. Listen. Feel. BE... and it is all there.

This is a journey that began before the beginning of time and continues beyond what we know as reality. Many souls, as one soul, united in our love of being. We allow ourselves to get caught up in the falseness, expectations and pressures from people and things outside ourselves. Take time to go deep inside the quiet recesses of our inner selves and there we will find truth. It is there where we will find our peace. Then our soul can rest and no longer have to try to keep living in a role that limits our being. It is in finding our own peace that others will be able to let go of the struggle and step outside the continued rehearsals of unhappy existence.

Shakespeare's words in As You Like It says that "All the world's a stage...", and so it is that each of us keep playing our roles and striving for perfection within these roles. Little do we know that the closer we come to perfection within these roles, the further we stray from truth and peace. Live in the moment. Feel what we feel. Be who we are, where we are. Our greatest reward does not come to us from heaven. We are our greatest reward and when we find ourselves, we have found heaven. Our identity lies not in the roles prescribed by a society that is lost from its course. Who we are lies within ourselves, within what we know to be true in our hearts.

August 30, 2003. The journey inward brings with it many questions and for a time, we are lost in a battle within ourselves. We are trying to know ourselves, and trying to hold on to everything we thought we knew about ourselves. During a time of great upheaval we begin to feel lost and at the same time so loved, unlike any love we have ever known. This in itself is so powerful. Feelings become clouded with doubts and questions. Is this the ego or is this true feeling?

The winds of change sweep across the land and across the ocean, as it also sweeps through my heart to transform my entire being. I have become so filled with love, with light, that it is difficult to establish my love from that which permeates my soul from outside sources, which really are one in the same. I questioned my own feelings, thought I was kidding myself. The ego played its role to the fullest. As I step further into the light and allow the love to shine, I am embracing not only myself, but also embracing all that the universe has designed for me. I made my sacred contract, and now ready to fulfill its promise, I continue to engage in humanness. How does humanness fit with divineness?

I have cried so many tears to release, cleanse, and raise myself to divineness. As one block releases, another presents itself so that piece by piece the truth becomes unraveled. The mysterious shroud, no longer so mysterious, is revealing itself. Whatever will humanity do when it no longer has a mystery to hold on to?

September 11, 2003. Love is something that we all desire and wish for in our lives. Yet, when we are faced with the promise of pure love, pure light, we fear it. What exactly is it that we fear? We reflect this fear from our ego; that place inside of us where our minds are caught up and enmeshed in the learning or modeling of our earthly and human experiences. We have seen fear, conflict, doubt, and this becomes our reference point against which we base all our knowledge. Our real knowing comes not from this reference point but from a deeper, heightened awareness beyond our physical mind. What we fear is ourselves. We are in awe of our own light. We view our lessons as part of the sacred contract but is it really part of the human will to remain in conflict? Perhaps we are not yet ready to let go of what we have understood to be part of this existence. It is easier to look upon another and offer them credit for the gifts they bring to us. We find it too difficult to see that the true gift comes from ourselves. We are each other and so, we can accept another's gift as our own gift to share and appreciate.

September 13, 2003. I sit at a crossroads and ask myself which way to turn. There is a knowingness of what is right and a knowingness of what my heart desires. The confusion lies in between.

I watch an empty chip bag blow across the beach and wonder... like the chip bag, evidence of our humanity, the letting go happens when we let the bag fall from our grasp for it no longer holds a purpose for us. It no longer contains anything we wish to consume. It is left free to be carried along by the breeze, wherever the breeze wishes to take it. We spend so much time asking questions about our life, about our direction. This is perhaps where the trouble lies. If we spent more time listening instead of asking, we would hear the answers and see the directions. We have agreed to be here to take on this challenge. It is up to us to decide where we go and when we stop the lessons. We are our own masters.

I spend so much time, so much energy in looking for "the one". Perhaps there is not just one but many. The great love I search for is truly within myself. We reach out and offer love to others and in so doing, offer it to ourselves. We have been limited in thinking that giving to others is giving away. The truth is that giving to others is giving to ourselves because it nurtures the spirit of oneness.

The fear of asking for what we want has limited our potential. From some place of feeling undeserving, we hold back. I am no longer afraid to ask for what I want. I want the universe and I have been receiving it. The universe is mine; it is yours. So now we need to own it. Own our divinity. Embrace our gifts. We are the masters. It is time to stop looking for answers outside of ourselves and go inward.

September 14, 2003

Dear Mom,

The time has come for forgiveness. I need to forgive you and to forgive myself for past mistakes and hurts. You also need to forgive yourself. I have known for a long time that you carry a burden for something, maybe for a lot of things that happened to you in your past. I have many guesses about what that is, but it is not for me to understand. It is you who needs to find that place within yourself and love yourself. Over the past few months, I have been on my own journey towards self-love and finally understand what is most important... complete self-love and acceptance.

There has been a great deal of conflict, tension, and stress over the years. It is time to let it all go. I am not telling you that we are going to have a picture-perfect or ideal relationship. I am not sure that we will ever have anything more than what we have right now. What I am telling you is that I understand more than you think about how difficult your life has been. I also understand that as much as you love your children, you were faced with responsibilities in your life and in your marriage that you did not necessarily want or feel prepared to take on. We all face things in our lives that we don't want to face but sometimes circumstances force us to deal with it the best we know how.

I have learned a great deal from you about what it means to be a mother, and to be forced to deal with unpleasant circumstances. Yes, I have faced many hurts and disappointments. I am letting it go because I need to release the pain in order to be happy within myself. It is my hope that you will be able to look deep within yourself and be completely honest with who you are and what you want, and most importantly to recognize love for yourself. If you don't first love yourself, then everything outside of you will not be able to bring you happiness. It will all be nothing more than an illusion, a false image of what you want to be true.

I see the hurt and pain in you. Even behind the fake smiles, I know that you are not happy with your life. I am telling you this because I know from my own experience over the past few months that your happiness will only be found when you start to look deep inside yourself and love yourself. Forgive your mistakes, forgive your wrong choices and start right now in this moment to love who you are. With every breath remind yourself that you are your own master. Your life is in your hands. Only you can bring happiness and joy to your life.

Mom, I do love you. It is difficult for me to admit this because there has been too much pain in my life. I was not able to love myself and to see myself reflected in you was too painful to bear. I have learned to love myself and because of that I am able to let go of the pain.

Please don't use this letter as means of pushing a closer bond to me. Use this letter for yourself... to look inside yourself and recognize an individual who is worthy of self-love and allow your light to shine. When you find your own sense of self-love, all that you desire from the universe will come to you. Everything you need to be happy is already there inside of you. Give yourself permission to accept it.

Love, Nancy

The healing with my father came through a healing letters workshop facilitated by a friend. We were instructed to write a letter to a person that we needed to heal a conflict with. My father seemed to be an obvious choice because even though I did not have any desire to be close to him again, I did want to release myself from the shame that held me back. The second part of this exercise was to write a letter from the perspective of the other person as if responding to the first letter. Wow...I didn't expect such an outpouring of compassion from this man. I think this was the first time I was truly able to see him as simply a man and not my father. He was a boy in a man's body. He was a boy wanting to be loved and accepted the same as I did. I'm not sure how or why but I felt the release happen. In months to follow, I was even finding myself wanting to visit him.

A Father's Day gathering with my siblings and their partners turned out to be an amazingly beautiful and joyful day. There was so much laughter and sharing and happiness to go around. As my dad hugged me and we posed for a picture to be taken, it seemed that all the years of disappointment had melted away. One day, purely in a moment of spontaneity, I hopped in my car and went to visit with him. He even allowed me to give him a Reiki treatment. It was a moment filled with such compassionate light and healing, as much for me as for him.

I found myself at a point in my life where I truly wanted to be healed from everything that was no longer serving me. I wanted release, and funny enough, it was my strong feelings of connection to Kathleen that triggered this desire to be released.

Unreal Love

October 2, 2003 ~ age 31

I've traveled down many roads

and distant paths

to find myself on the shore

of some uncertain fate.

Along the way

at some juncture unseen,

our paths did cross

and become a single path

towards a future predetermined.

A warm heart strengthened

and opened to the brilliant light.

My soul rejoiced at your presence

and basked in the glowing joy

of having found you,

only now I weep...

for every broken glance,

every sideways turn away from me.
To have been directed towards
and introduced to
such a deep and powerful love
only to be denied its embrace
is painful beyond words.
Only spirit can know the fate
of such a journey;
the purpose of such turmoil.
To grow from this
and become transformed
may be the purpose,
but how does my human heart
bear the agony of loving you
so deeply and so passionately,
but never being able to express it?

Into You

October 3, 2003 ~ age 31

I look to you
for hope, for love, for understanding,
for answers that
I cannot seem to find
within myself.
I search your eyes,
I hold your hand,
to feel connected,
to find a bridge.
I look into you
and I see...
I see myself.
all along
it was myself
that I sought to find.

Chapter Six

Awakening the Vision

For as long as I could remember, there was a sense of uneasiness with the whole idea of 'religion' and 'God'. I wasn't sure that any of it was believable, at least not the way I had been hearing about it. There had to be something more to it. A conversation with two of my college friends stirred up some of these questions. We explored our ideas on reincarnation, alien life, ghosts, and metaphysics. It was the first real discussion that seemed to make some sense to me. I still didn't fully comprehend my own beliefs but something in all this set off a tinge of familiarity in knowing that there's more than what our human eyes can see. As we were just starting to get deeply enthralled into the discussion, some of the others girls came into the room to see what we were talking about. Our enlightened conversation stopped pretty quickly in the presence of rebuttal and scorn. We never did get to finish that exploration because we all felt too overwhelmed by the lack of acceptance. I certainly didn't want to chance being rejected again, especially when I was finally starting to find a place of acceptance.

Now that the years had passed and comfortableness came with expressing my own ideas, a new place of acceptance welcomed me. This new spiritual life erupted with an excitement and enthusiasm that I had never known before. Questioning everything about my life and about myself was leading me to a deeper wisdom about my own journey and a greater awareness of oneness, of All that Is.

As I learned more about this energy that seems to connect everything and started to feel the beautiful flow of life, I treated myself with love and nourished my sense of deserving and of being worthy. Thoughts starting coming about being capable of creating anything I wanted and deserving to have it. Driving out over the road one sunny morning, a thought popped into my head. Just for fun, I decided to take out a new car for a test drive. It seemed like an innocent enough way to have a bit of fun. The next morning, I was driving in to Mazda to pick up my new car. It was the beginning of a new journey for me. As silly as it sounds, it came to me in a dream to give my car the name Ariel. I figured that since Archangel Ariel watched over me through my spiritual journey, my car would watch over my many journeys on the road in my travels to new adventures. As much as any material object could be adored, my car became my love, carrying me through spiritual conversations on leisurely drives, to workshops and road trips to visit family or with friends. The universe blessed me with my first sign of new abundance.

Included in this abundance was a widening circle of friends which came through the gatherings for meditation. Powerful energies were infusing into me and through me, and connected me with other beings of light. I attribute a great deal of my growth to these meditative gatherings where we shared our insights, our experiences, and lovingly supported each other through our processes of waking up.

I began to meet many of my soul mates and started recognizing the love that abounds in the universe. I started to feel completely at one with this life energy, at one with me, the real me. Then the prophetic dreams, visions, and insights started to come to me. At first it was kind of freaking me out, especially when the dreams manifested before me, and then there were the cryptic dreams that sometimes really boggled me. Slowly over the course of the next year, I settled into a willingness and acceptance to embrace this energy and learned to work within the principles of Divine Timing. The awe-inspiring ability of energy to transform, transmute, and transport my spiritual essence to other dimensions manifested in my daily life.

New teachers presented to me and I began to accept the pureness of love that comes in the oneness of the light. It would only be over the course of the next year that my deep connection and love for these soul mates would manifest. I met my Sister in Spirit at a seminar and immediately felt warmth in my heart for her, as if we had known each other forever. It seemed that a number of synchronistic events had brought us together, and it was certainly part of the Divine Plan for us to meet.

As my friendship with Stefanie grew, I started to gain a deeper appreciation for her ability to stay connected and grounded through anything. She had a way of reaching people in such a gentle and loving way. I grew to love the way she could find humour in everything and lighten up even the most seemingly depressing situation.

I started reaching out to Stefanie in an effort to resolve the confusion over the visions and also to seek resolution to the troubling matters of the heart. There was a comfortable space between us that allowed me to share many of my innermost thoughts and feelings, even the ones that were very embarrassing to me. She always listened with patience, compassion, and without judgment. Sometimes I felt an almost maternal bond between us, and there were even times when I wanted to cry like a baby while she held me in her arms. Her mere presence somehow helped to keep me focused

Stefanie introduced me to A *Course in Miracles*, at least in a more formal way. I had heard about this book before and was curious but never seemed to find my way to it. I had always been a little put off by any texts that made references to God and still wasn't entirely sure of my acceptance of it. The idea of having to follow a rule book on how to be saved made me a little nervous. Nonetheless, she helped me to sort out the real from the unreal and to gain deeper wisdom from within. More than that, she mirrored my recognition of the wisdom that was already residing within. I had no idea when I first met her how instrumental she would be in my spiritual awakening.

My Sister in Spirit mirrored so much of myself and served as such a loving witness as I reached further into my oneness of Being. She showed me through her own example, how truly perfect and joyful and peaceful it is to simply BE. Again The Course in Miracles offered a perfect description of what I was witnessing in this beautiful soul. She was with me through all that would unfold over the coming months, and continues to be with me now. As much as I came to recognize that all connections between God's children are special, I still hold her in a very dear place in my heart where few have ever reached.

Around the same time, Spirit guided into a mentorship with another beautiful light that would open me up to far greater insights and awareness than I could ever have imagined. I had met Sam many years ago when he was a neighbour to my sister, Rebecca. I never got to really know him, just knew of him being around. He seems to be a little bit of an enigma. At times I feel completely baffled by him, not sure whether to run from him or to embrace him. He has a very commanding presence in spite of his unassuming stature and small build.

Sam serves as another mirror to me and inspires me to reach to the depths of my faith and beyond. He helped me face some of my fears of trusting, of setting my boundaries, and of expressing myself. We have had many long talks about the trials we've faced and the importance of holding on to our faith. Sam is an amazing man in many ways, and underneath it all, he is a human being with his follies, just like the rest of us. He has allowed me to see into his heart and has embraced me. I see the child-like innocence in him as well as the mighty power. Eventually I was able to open my heart to allow him in. He mirrored for me the difficulties that present when we allow ourselves to be caught up in the turmoil of battling between ego and Spirit.

In the span of only a year, I went from being a quiet, isolated, sad and weary soul to being a Deva, a Goddess, a beautiful and vibrant woman. I started to really love myself, love my energy, and love how it felt to be freely enjoying life. My circle of friends multiplied. My style of dress changed. Feeling radiant inside and out, people I had known suddenly didn't recognize me. A co-worker commented on the glow about me and that even my eyes seemed to have come to life. I felt that not only was my spirit changing, but also my physical body and my mind. I started to really notice things around me, a noticing that went beyond the appearances of things. My human eyes were transforming into spiritual eyes. It became my mission to dive into my new career path as an Energy Healer and Light Worker.

As I took steps away from the safety of my first new home in the light, and away from the ties to my first teacher, I put my faith in the universe to guide me on my path. I was feeling sad about leaving the security and comfort of the group, but recognized my growing dependence on them. It was holding me back. I felt inside that it was time to find my own way, even with the uncertainty of what would come for me, or how it would come. As usually happens as soon as you let go, the universe comes rushing in to fill your desire for something new. A chance meeting led me towards receiving my attunements that would officially make me a Reiki Healer. As I worked through this training and continued to explore meditative practices, I quickly recognized that there were greater adventures in store for me.

Mirrored Souls

November 2, 2003 ~ age 31

We started on a journey toward ourselves
and found each other along the way.
We find in one another a mirrored reflection
of all that we have yearned for
and also what we have feared.
We see images of such profound beauty
and find ourselves looking away
because its intensity stirs in us
feelings that we do not understand
and are not sure that we are worthy of.
Slowly, gently, our soul begins its awakening.
We begin to truly see and understand
our own beauty, our own worthiness.
The fears we carry slowly melt away
into knowingness and acceptance.
In recognition of our common journey
we are now able to face one another,
as we face ourselves,
in true recognition
of our humanity and our divinity.

Chapter Seven

A Whole New World

During the course of my training, I experienced another one of those soul mate encounters. Looking into eyes that flooded me with feelings of deep affection left me shaken, not only because of the turmoil caused by my last soul mate encounter, but also because of the uncertainty of being ready for a potentially real relationship. I resisted Miriam for many weeks, fearful of allowing my heart to hang out there only to be rejected again. I couldn't stop what was happening, nor could I ignore my heart telling me to be with her. Miriam was a free spirit, delightful and playful. She was beautiful with her long, flowing hair, clear-blue eyes, and when she danced, her body flowed so gracefully in tune with the energies. She was fragile, yet amazingly strong, awkward at times, but very graceful in her connection with spirit. She would often sing to me, with her sweet, soothing voice reaching the depths of my heart. No one ever sang to my heart like she did. She even wrote songs for me. I truly felt like a goddess.

Sweet Surprise

January 27, 2004

I see you on some distant shore.

I recognize you, yet I don't know you.

My eyes meet your gaze

and in some way, it fills me.

Like a ray of light into shadows,

your presence seeps into my heart.

Your laughter sings to my soul

as a familiar and cherished melody.

I begin to know you

and begin to recognize you

inside myself.

Miriam and I talked openly about where our hearts were, both of us carrying some fresh wounds. Opening my heart to love again was very refreshing. It was the first actual relationship I experienced with another enlightened being. It was exciting, intense, joyful, and at times very difficult. It helped me to stretch beyond myself.

Our relationship intensified very quickly with the recognition that something stronger than us had brought us together. We seemed to support each other in a way that neither of us had known before. I deeply appreciated Miriam's willingness to share freely what was happening in her heart and to listen without judgment for what was happening in mine. Starting this relationship posed another set of considerations. She was on the verge of leaving the country. I had a tough decision to make.

Initially, my reservations told me to stay with my life here, that when and if she returned, we would then know if this relationship was for real. I wasn't sure of my ability to handle another broken romance. Something in my heart pulled me and despite the screaming logic in my mind, I made the huge leap of faith to drop everything and go to India. Some part of me knew that this journey had little, if anything, to do with this relationship and everything to do with me.

The Fool

February 2004

Towards destiny's calling,

into the river flow,

casting off worries

and the armour of illusions.

Unknown valleys.

Unknown plains.

I travel with my own guide

against all that would dub me

the fool.

We prepared for out trip to India with much excitement and got swept up in a flurry of the intense emotions. We decided that we would get married while we were away, and upon our return we would carry on with building a life together in Israel, her home soil. Our friends gathered around to support us and share in the sheer bliss we were feeling. We were inspired in so many ways and believed fully that all our dreams were manifesting. It almost seems silly to me now because that dream was so short lived. At the time, however, the feelings were very real for both of us.

This chapter in my book of lessons began the moment I stepped unto Indian soil. At the Delhi airport swarms of taxi drivers wait outside the gates, all of them desperate to grab the next promise of money in their pocket. It was astounding to me to be caught in a mass of shouting and scrambling, with me at the center. I suppose it could have been seen as an honour to have all these people fighting for the privilege of carrying my bags. I should have felt like royalty, but instead wanted to scream. Feeling so tired from the fifteen hours of flying, the last thing that was needed was to face a mob. This would become something that was faced at every corner. I never did fully learn to deal with the feeling of being an object representing someone's conquest. For now, though, Miriam willingly took charge.

The two hour taxi ride allowed a moment to relax and simply take it all in. The blur of traffic, street signs and the store window advertisements offered a sort of meditation. It was surprising to see so much American influence in the billboards. I suppose I had an expectation that India would be removed from the rest of the world. It was also amazing to see such little regard for traffic rules and how drivers competed for a space in the road. It seemed like a much-amplified version of American road rage. It made me laugh and it refreshed my appreciation for being able to have leisurely drives on the highway.

It is next to impossible to describe my impressions of India, at least in any way of doing justice to the true experience of it. The essence of it can only be experienced in the sights, sounds, smells, and energy that buzzed around me and through me. Over the course of the six weeks I spent listening to the people's stories, observing their festivals, and witnessing the pulse of the daily routines, something inside me shifted. I gained a keener awareness of the sanctity of human experience. A simple walk down the street easily changed from serenity and sweet-smelling flowers to sudden brutality, chaos, and the grunge of garbage, human refuse and dead dogs left in the middle of the road after being run over. Then there was the quiet reverence along the shores of the rivers, and the vibrant garments and banners flying in the temples. Amidst the celebrations, the scuffles, and the mists floating above the trees at dawn, I looked into the eye of the needle that sewed its threads through my life. In some crazy, mixed-up yet simple way, my life started to make sense.

One day we went to visit one of the holy pools in the center of town. It is believed that these pools were built by Krishna for his bride Rhada. People go there to bathe and splash the water over them as a blessing from Krishna. Miriam and I stood by the water's edge and held each other's hand. We looked into each other's eyes and saw heaven. It was truly a beautiful moment. I felt that the Spirit of Krishna and of Rhada, and of All That Is, had offered a blessing. To even be standing there, in that place, at that moment, was a miracle in itself.

A little girl had started following us. She was so tiny and sweet and innocent, not like the other kids who were chasing us trying every trick to get our money. She was wearing a lilac dress, dusty from the roads. She was barefoot and I noticed the calluses and scrapes on her feet and legs. She couldn't have weighed more than 20 pounds at six years old. She looked up with her deep, dark eyes and smiled. Miriam took a hold of the little girl's hand while I took the other, and the three of us walked together around the pool.

We sat by the pool's edge and I gave the little girl a granola bar that was in my purse. At first she held it in her hands with wide eyes looking upon this strange treasure with its sparkly wrapper. She didn't seem to know what to do with it, so Miriam opened it up for her. She carefully ate a tiny piece and then offered to share it. She didn't speak a word of English and I spoke no Hindi, but somehow between the three of us, we communicated in a lovely exchange. We found out her name was Lilam. Sitting there on those steps, the three of us together, breathing in the energy of this mystical place, I felt hope that it was actually possible to have happiness.

We walked through the street together, still holding hands. Occasionally Lilam would point something out, as if being our tour guide. We laughed and skipped along feeling carefree. We stopped at a treat shop to buy some sweets. Some of the other kids had found their way back to us and created a scene around us. Lilam became very insistent, trying to get our attention. Miriam told me to ignore it; that it was just a ploy to get more money or treats. We continued on our way, with Lilam and me walking slightly behind. She looked up at me and quietly spoke to me again, trying to explain. As my eyes met her dark and intense gaze, I finally understood what she was telling me. She tried to warn us that the man at the shop was overcharging us for the sweets. We should have listened to her. I thanked her and she smiled at me with appreciation. My heart was so full of love for this little girl. I wanted to take her home with me. I've often wondered about her since leaving India. She really wasn't like the others. She had a sparkle shining brightly in her soul. I knew that if I ever have a little girl of my own, her name would be Lilam.

It seems very strange to me how events unfolded in the course of my journey in India. I went there full of excitement and anticipation of my exciting travels in this strange new world. I was so pumped up on the thrill of starting my new life with my beloved. The first couple of weeks was a time of extreme physical illness, adjusting to the food and the environment, and also adjusting to the strong energies working through me to transmute and released the deep, dark parts of myself that had been buried. I was so weakened at times that I thought I would just have to allow myself to collapse in the floor until gaining enough strength to go on. It was a weakening of all my defences.

Only two short weeks after we left Canada, things started to crumble down around me. My relationship with Miriam came to a screeching halt. Miriam came to me very excited about having received some great insight or prophetic vision. She proceeded to lay out the cards before me and explain how our personalities are clashing. That night as I looked into her eyes, I was jolted by the darkness I saw there. Where did those beautiful blue pools of light go? They were replaced by pure blackness that shook me at my core. It was not Miriam's eyes I looked into but some other dark creature that I did not recognize. The Miriam that I fell in love with was no longer there. I prayed that night for protection from whatever this dark force was that had moved in. As I lay in dream state that evening, I saw a vision of a huge dark shadow with glaring eyes and teeth moving toward me. My prayers for protection produced glowing hands reaching out to lift me from this shadow and my heart swelled with gratitude. In this lucid state, I recalled lessons from The Course in Miracles that reminded me that I could only be attacked if I chose to believe that it was real. In this moment I brought in the acceptance and forgiveness for having forgotten my strength as a Divine Being. With this, I turned around to face the dark demon and as I did, it started to shrink away from me and dissipated. My heart rejoiced for having remembered who I am.

Miriam and I chose to try to support each other lovingly through this transition. We continued to travel across India and into the Himalayas for about another month. It was an experience like those I had only read about in books and thought it could never happen to me. It was really something not of this world. There were energies moving through me and around me that was literally transforming me, leading me through my first real death.

I had been slowly dying over a period of time leading up to this but had not been fully aware of it, at least not in the sense of a spiritual death. Piece by piece parts of my illusion were falling away. Then one day, sitting on a bench under some trees in a private courtyard, a flash of insight came. Listening to the sounds and smelling the various scents in the air was surreal. I watched the evening sun reflecting off the leaves fluttering in the breeze and felt like I was floating away with it. The realization of my death was coming to me. The self that I had known was suddenly recognized as a complete façade. It was a shadow casting doubts and fears into the brilliant light shining underneath. In that very instance, I knew there would never be a return to the self that I had known.

Thoughts of my mother came as I recalled how so many people had spoken of us having the same eyes. I could never look into her eyes for the sadness and pain that was seen there. Kathleen had once commented on me having my mother's eyes. I squirmed when she said it. Now I wondered if that's why Kathleen couldn't look into my eyes, the same as I couldn't look into my mother's. Perhaps Kathleen was fearful of falling into my eyes as I had fallen into hers so long ago. For me to look into my mother's eyes was to see a mirror of my own pain. The shock of this realization stirred something deep inside me and I knew it had to be shared with my mother in order to release my own pain and forgive myself. I hoped it could do the same for her.

The Flow

March 16, 2004

Drifting past, drifting into,
falling through a chasm
of unknown fate.
Like a river flowing,
carried away weightlessly,
letting go.
Layers wash away
cleansing deeper
into the essence of self.
Who I am, who I was,
no longer the same.
Changing perceptions,
purging of inner demons
re-creating self
into pureness of truth.

I cannot in any way adequately describe to the cleansing and purging process that worked through me during my time in India. There was a complete transformational energy that swept through every layer of my being; physical, emotional, intellectual, and spiritual. On a daily basis opportunities were presented to let go into the flow of life.

It was also a letting go of the relationship that had just started. My relationship with Miriam had served its purpose in a continued unleashing of the shadows that lay buried inside of me. The remaining weeks of my travels became a time of emerging out of the shadows and an opportunity to step closer into the light of my own soul.

We found a guesthouse to stay for a while, to allow a rest to absorb the energy shifts happening. It was lovely place with a rooftop restaurant and a large open space where we could sit to meditate, to write, or to dance. In the early mornings, it was refreshing to sit and watch the birds flying about the flowering trees before heading off to the markets to partake of the vibrant displays of every kind of fruit and vegetable imaginable. I had never before seen such vibrant colors of food. And the fruit were always so tantalizingly sweet in their freshness and ripeness. It became a sort of game to try something new every day. The fresh vegetable and fruit salads that we'd make were a heavenly meal to enjoy in the shade of the rooftop while the midday heat sweltered outside. Our fresh salads became quite a huge hit among the other guests who would sometimes enjoy the meal with us.

It was always too hot to go anywhere in the middle of the day, so this became the time for rest, reading, and meditating. I spent many long hours sitting on that rooftop, especially in the evenings when the temperatures settled to a bearable warmth. It offered a breathtaking view of an ancient fort, towering above the whole city. At night, it would be lit up with the floodlights to make it appear as a sort of mirage. As I stared into the lights and absorbed the ancient energy of this fort, it seemed to transport me through time. Sometimes, I even had the feeling of being held captive in that fort, looking out through the bars of the window, longing to be free.

I had a wonderfully powerful journey with the light angels on this rooftop. Miriam and I sat there together one evening, preparing for a distance Reiki treatment for some loved ones back home in Newfoundland. I felt myself releasing from my physical body and saw the two us being lifted on the wings of the angels and carried through the air in a swirling motion. We were infused with a blue-white light and became part of a beautifully orchestrated dance of oneness with the light. Then, as I was carried further into this light, Miriam was carried away from me and disappeared in the opposite direction. The place where I found myself was beyond what my senses could describe.

Kathleen was there waving her hand for me to come to her. Turning to face her, I felt the weight of emotions that has passed between us. She motioned again for me to come closer and it seemed that I was finally being allowed a glimpse into her heart. I tried to speak with her but she seemed to not be able to speak to me in words. She looked up at me, held my hand and there were tears rolling gently from her eyes. Through a heartlink, we were able to offer each other some comfort and reassurance. It seemed that she was trying to tell me something but couldn't find the words. I thanked her for being there, for allowing me to share this moment and then I told her it was time for me to move on. I felt the sadness that she couldn't tell me what she needed to tell me. I wanted so much to hear the truth, but somehow my heart already knew the truth. Everything was as it needed to be. The angels then carried me back through this portal of light and ever so gently guided me back into my body. After that journey, I always felt the desire to keep dancing.

One night I was there alone on my rooftop and danced for hours to unleash the expression I was feeling in my heart, feeling at one with my body and all the emotions welling up from deep inside. I danced through my sadness, my anger, my bitterness, and into my feelings of pure joy. I looked up and noticed that people were watching me from a nearby hotel but didn't care. My self-consciousness seemed to float away. I felt happy and content, totally oblivious to the fact that Miriam was downstairs in our room sleeping and coming closer to a big decision that would alter the course of our lives together.

About a week later, we had headed west toward the border of Pakistan. I was blessed with an opportunity to spend a night sleeping in the desert at Jaisalmer, where the stars shone so brilliantly at night and were so numerous that it felt as if I could simply reach out and scoop them up into my hands. The coolness that settled over the sand dunes at night was a direct contrast to the scorching heat of the day. In the pureness of night, unobstructed by the glare of streetlights, I beheld the majesty of the sky. It was enthralling to see how the sky could be so richly imbued with stars. I enjoyed the feel of the sand trickling between my toes and soaked in the essence of peacefulness around me. Miriam and I rolled around in the sand, trying to make sand angels, just like I had shown her to make snow angels in the park back home. When it started to get dark, the very air became saturated with stillness unlike anything I could imagine. Miriam crawled up onto the dune where I was sitting and nestled herself close to me. She draped her arms across my legs and allowed her head to rest on my chest. I drank in the sweet smell of her hair and hugged her close to me. It was a perfect moment. We settled into the silence that blanketed us and drowned out everything, even the thoughts pushing their way through my mind. It was as if we were drawn into a void.

I had been warned about the scorpions that could be found there, and experienced first-hand the sand beetles tunnelling up through the sand and between my toes. The real fears weren't of the creepy crawlies of the night. I felt more alarmed by the recognition of truth slowly seeping into my awareness, a match for the chill of the night air of the desert. It was here in this place that Miriam finally told me the truth of what was hiding in her heart; the fears she had of committing to a life-long partnership. She was a free spirit. One of the things I most admired about her was also one of the things that prevented us from being able to stay together. She held me while the gut wrenching sorrows spilled over what was to be yet another lost love. Still, she hadn't been able to find it in her to let me go just yet.

The next morning, so early that the sun was barely finding its way over the horizon, I climbed up the sand dunes to find the perfect place to greet the sun. Engaging in my usual morning rituals of embracing the morning and stretching into my body, the energies flowed through me to allow some reassurance. It usually rejuvenated me and gave me the focus to carry on, but on this particular morning, the heaviness didn't leave me. Sitting there in the dune, high up above everything, I prayed for my peace. It would come, slowly and gently working its way through my soul as I walked along the shores of the Ganga and trekked through the mountainsides of the Himalayas.

Long ago in middle school history class, I had learned a little about the rituals that unfold daily on the shores of the Ganga. Now it was right here in front of me. My first day in Varanasi brought me to a guesthouse with a balcony overlooking the site where the bodies were burned before being dumped into the river. Looking back on it now, I realize the symbolic message in being so near the grounds of consecrating the passage from life into physical death and release into the light. Miriam sheltered me from this image and suggested we go to another guesthouse. She felt reasonably sure I wouldn't want to be trying to sleep next to the site of such release. I was thankful to have not witnessed it so close but it permeated the air all around us. We found another place that was perfectly suited to both of us.

We had a balcony that opened up directly beside a rooftop of an abandoned dwelling. There were trees sheltering us and in the late afternoons, this provided a beautiful repose from the noisy street. I swept off the rooftop and climbed across to it to dance and do my Qi Gong exercises. It was lovely. I also got to share it with groups of monkeys who would swing down from the trees. Of course we couldn't share it at the same time. These monkeys, although fairly indifferent to human company, couldn't be trusted, especially if there was food around.

One really hot day I was resting on my bed. Before I knew it, the door flew open and a monkey came flying in. The cheeky lad was coming back to see what other treasures it could find after having already stolen something from the window ledge. Here it was again, determined to get what it wanted. I had to shout at it to get it to leave. Apparently only loud banging or shouting wildly is enough to scare them off. I was kind of glad to have an opportunity to scream and release some of the tensions being held in my body.

I managed to get the monkey to leave and locked the door behind him, but he didn't give up easily. He kept beating at the door trying to get in. He eventually gave up, but then came a gentler one accompanied by a baby one. They sat outside my window with me only a couple of feet away. It was amazing to be so close to them and look into their eyes. We sat there and shared some biscuits in a wordless communication. The tiny fingers of this baby ever so cautiously reached out for the treat. It was if they understood when the biscuits were all gone. The older one grunted at me with disgust and went off. The baby lingered with a pitiful expression as if pleading for more. Then it rolled its eyes and went on its way. I chuckled over that confrontation for hours later. In a symbolic sense, the monkeys on my back weren't quite ready to leave me alone. I was still carrying the traces of doubts about what was waiting for me when I returned home.

Every day in Varanasi revolved around the Ganga, one of three holy rivers said to flow from Shiva's crown. To bathe in its waters or receive a blessing is an honour that the people go to its shores daily to receive. At first I didn't see it because I was too caught up in what was seen on the surface; people bathing in a polluted river where dead people's ashes floated by. As the days stretched by, the scenes started to play out in a slow murmur of consequential instances. One evening in particular, I watched through the darkness as a line of lights slowly edged along the distant shore. It was a funeral possession with the people carrying candles that eventually were placed on the water to be carried along with the current. These candles were offered as a blessing to honour all life. These shores were a continuous bombardment of people mourning, celebrating, singing, dancing, bathing, doing laundry, bartering with tourists, sipping Chai and reading their papers. It was amazing to me. There was a reverence for the cycle of life.

One day we hired a boat to go on the river. It was later in the evening and the lights were reflecting off the water. We could also see hundreds of flickering candlelights from the floating candles on the water. I had a tiny stone in my hand. A friend had given it to me before I left for India. She had asked me to take this tiny piece of Newfoundland and when it felt right, leave it somewhere as a gesture to connect the energies of Newfoundland to India. The Ganga river seemed like such a place. It was a place where all life comes together, the people, the animals, and the souls of those who are released once again into All That Is. As the tiny stone slipped from my hand into the depths of the river, a gentle yet powerful stirring moved through my soul to offer me a glimpse of the journey yet to come.

India

March 15, 2004

It lies there beyond imagination
into eyes that know depths
of reaching souls across time.
It shows us worlds unknown
with it's chaotic blend
of riches and poverty,
where humans and creatures
each find their place.
It shines with untouchable beauty
in it's harmony of being.

We went from the river and headed into tea country, Darjeeling. It was breathtakingly beautiful so high up into the mountains, far removed from the heat and pollution of the country. My days were filled with strolling along hillsides; breathing in the fresh mountain air, visiting the Buddhist temple, and watching the fog roll in and out. I would sit on the balcony of our guesthouse and look out into the fog, which was so thick at times that I couldn't see beyond my hands reach. The hotel sat on the side of a steep hill, so when it was foggy, the balcony would seemingly be left suspended in the mists. I felt as if I were existing somewhere between worlds, hovering in the mists. Sometimes I could imagine being lifted up and carried on a journey through that fog. Many hours were spent on that balcony, going deeper inside myself, savouring every morsel of life and taking nourishment in the Tibetan bread with jam that reminded me of toutons from home. It was comforting to me in a time of feeling completely uprooted.

Darjeeling was the longest stay, offering a beautiful, refreshing sanctuary while we both waited for some guidance to come as to our next move. We both needed the time and space to sort through what was happening to us. I developed a daily ritual of having Thukpa, a Tibetan noodle soup at a local Nepalese restaurant where the owners seemed to become my friends. They would call out and wave as I walked down the street. This became a meeting place for Miriam and me, since we were now spending our days on solitary exploration. At this restaurant, we had many great conversations about the way of life of Darjeeling and how the town developed over the years.

Then there was the old lady at the craft shop. I would go in there every day to admire her knitted socks and sweaters, and mostly just to enjoy her presence. I guessed she was around eighty years old. She always wore her hair pulled back in a bun, and always donned the traditional work dress of Nepali woman. She had a very gentle, welcoming presence, and we would talk back and forth, not really understanding a single word. Still, she gave me her big smile with eyes sparkling when she looked up. She had one tooth missing, and the lines around her face spoke of the years of laughter and smiles. I bought some of her woollen socks to wear. It was so much colder in the high altitudes of the Himalayas. I still wear those woollen socks now, and am always reminded of the sweet lady that made them.

For five days, I trekked through the mountain trails that found their way through several tiny mountain villages. Many of these villages consisted of no more than two or three families. I was astounded at the simplicity of their life and the profound sense of peace and contentment. These mountain people never seemed to be upset and went about their daily routines with joyfulness. In their faces, I could see so much connection to life and to living. It was almost as if I could read their stories in the lines of their faces, and their eyes were so deep and dark, yet shining with love.

One old lady, now close to ninety, still offered her rooms to Trekkers. We would all sit on little stools, huddled around her oven with her daughter translating for us to have some conversation with her. She would be up with the sunrise to offer us a morning tea to enjoy as we greeted mists still lingering above the hills. Even the villagers still took a moment each morning to appreciate the beauty of it.

Trekking through these mountains with the woman I loved, knowing by now that we were going our separate ways upon our return, was the most powerful experience I had ever encountered. It was five long days of walking meditation, going deeper inside with every step. Most of the journey, I walked alone. Miriam wanted to be with herself, and so we walked with a about a half mile gap between us. I felt that she had already left me and I was on this journey through the forests and jungles on my own with only my thoughts and the endless stretch of the mysteries of the mountains to keep me company. Like the footprints in the sand, I trekked on with growing awareness of Spirit guiding my steps.

There's no way for me to adequately describe the overwhelming sense of being a tiny speck of life as I took in the scenery of sprawling mountainside and was surrounded by nothing but the sounds of the forest and my own heart beating in my chest. Hiking through fog, rain, hail, snow, sunshine and rainbows was the most profound affirmation of life I could have ever experienced. Under mountain streams blessings and gratitude were offered to Spirit and to my angels who assisted me along the way. Some places felt like it may have been the hiding place of the fairies of the forest. I connected again with the child inside of me that I had long forgotten.

At one point on this journey, I rounded the corner and saw a message in the sand that fell down from the hillside. It wasn't a message in the sense that most people would think of it, but when I feasted my eyes upon this image, tremendous joy filled my heart. Prior to leaving for India, I had been receiving some guidance and assistance from a Reiki Practitioner who was helping me sort through some of my emotional issues. A great deal of effort was put into balancing and connecting the energies of my head and my heart. Now, here I was, thousands of miles away from home, and before me in the sand was the image of a heart that someone had etched in the sand, and across from it, the skull of a bull. At first I laughed in the recognition of my bull-headedness and then the powerful energy of this message started to seep in. It was a miraculous confirmation of being right where I needed to be.

There were literally hundreds of enlightened moments along this mountain trail. I could not possibly share all of them; not sure I even remember the details of most of them, but the energy of it left its signature upon my soul. I had often heard the reference to taking the higher road of Spirit. This resonated with me very deeply one afternoon on my walk through a wooded section of the trail. I was surrounded and almost completely shrouded in flowering rhododendron trees. The fragrance of these flowers lingered so thick in the air that I became the air itself. Stopping often just to drink it in and allow myself to be lost in it, I welled up with the emotions that had been locked away. I allowed the hurt, the anger and the disappointment of my relationship to sink in. So many tears came and then the silence of merely breathing it in.

I looked down and watched a while as Miriam was winding her way up through the trees. Remembering those words that Stefanie had often reminded me of, "Take the high road", I suddenly felt much better in making a choice to embrace the experience of what was happening. Somehow my soul would rise above the emotions to find a place of peace within myself, a place of truly recognizing the gift of this experience. I found that place of peace within my heart, because regardless of the emotions, I did see the realness of love. I climbed up on a huge boulder and stood there looking out over the expanse of mountains. Feeling truly empowered, I shouted out "I'm the queen of the world".

As my walk continued, a clump of flowers had fallen from the trees into the middle of my path. I picked them up to smell them. For a moment I thought about waiting to give them to Miriam, but then decided it was best to leave them on the trail. It was enough to have the recognition within my own heart of what it meant. I filled those flowers with my appreciation and then laid them down. A few minutes later I glanced back to see that Miriam had stopped to pick up those same flowers and breathed them in, just as I had done. A knowingness settled into my heart that regardless of what had come between us, we were blessed with a beautiful light that connected us always.

Somewhere towards the summit of that mountain range, a metamorphosis happened inside of me. Physically climbing those mountains, I was surpassing myself and letting go with every step. My attention became focused on each stone that supported me in my climb. I thought that along our path there might be dozens of stepping-stones to choose from. We choose one that feels right and then carry on. Someone else may choose differently. In the end, we all come out to the same place to celebrate having reached the summit. That is such a true reflection of life; of the people we meet along the way, and the experiences we have. Each one of them gives us something that adds to the beauty of it all.

I descended the other side of that mountain as a completely different person. Something had washed through me and I felt it in my soul that I would never be the same. Perhaps the mandala image that had come to me in a meditation earlier that year was a premonition. This Mandela had shown me a blue butterfly with mountains in the background. Now here I was descending from the Himalayas feeling as though I were emerging from my chrysalis. A few weeks ago I also watched a movie called *The Blue Butterfly* and again I saw the message in it for me…that the wondrous blue butterfly that we all seek is an enigma. The so-called butterfly, or the miracle, is the beauty that is in all life. It surrounds us in everything we see and hear and breathe. We waste our time trying to capture something that seems to elude us when all along it right there in front of us. We don't see it because we have an expectation of its form.

Over the few days of resting in a mountain lodge, my own inner voice started to tell me it's time to go home. The decision was made that upon returning to Darjeeling, I would be boarding a train and heading back to Delhi, and back to my Newfoundland, with or without my traveling companion. As it turned out, Miriam decided from some sense of responsibility for my safety, to make the return trip with me. Initially, anger flared that she wouldn't just let me go but that soon waned when I thought about having to battle on my own for boundaries in a train car filled with men who drooled over American women.

Once I made my decision to return to Canada, it seemed the universe shifted on my behalf. A flight became available almost immediately which meant being able to avoid the long painful wait for my departure. I filled my time with some shopping and making peace with my early departure.

It was in the few remaining hours left in India that a messenger greeted me. At the time, I suppose I was too tired of the games that happened in the street, the battle for space and boundaries. I didn't fully allow what this man tried to tell me. He was standing in the middle of the road, amid the chaos of the street. He looked oddly out of place, dressed in a white suit and headdress just like many middle-aged men in India wear. It was odd that he appeared so bright and clean compared to everyone else. Most people are dusty from the roads. As I approached, pushing my way through the crowd, he turned to walk towards me. It seemed as if he had waited there just for me. I brushed him aside as I learned to with many of the people accosting tourists for money or business ventures. He left.

When I came back up the street, there he was again, trying to speak to me as before, saying. "Please, there's something I need to tell you". Again, I brushed him aside. That same evening he was there again, same as before. This time I figured I had better speak to him, because he seemed very intent on getting my attention. I stopped and turned to face him and said, "Okay, what is so important for you to tell me?" He looked into my eyes and I became transfixed in his. He spoke directly to my soul, saying, "What do I have to tell you? No, it's what you have to understand". I started to turn away; feeling like this is just too crazy. He followed me asking almost desperately, "What are you searching for in your life?" I asked him why he was trying so hard to talk to me and he stopped in front of me, again looking intently into my eyes. He told me I am not a stupid woman, and then again asked with greater conviction, "What are you searching for in your life?" As I walked away from him, I hesitated, feeling mixed feelings whether to stay or go. I turned around to see him again, but he was gone. He seemed to have just disappeared.

Three months would pass before I would have a full grasp of the meaning of that encounter. One evening, sitting at the desk at work, it came to me. I grabbed my pen again and started writing before this moment of clarity escaped me.

July 28, 2004 *"What are you searching for in your life?" That was a question a stranger kept asking me. I didn't realize at the time how very important that question would be. I suppose I could say it changed my life. It made me realize that I was searching for something outside myself, something unattainable outside myself. As we stood there in the street, looking into each other's eyes, and as I asked him to tell me what he wanted to tell me, I began to realize that I was looking at myself. The eyes I was searching into were my own. I shook my head and walked away and I realize now it was because I wasn't ready to understand. I've often questioned why I didn't stay and hear him out. . .what would he have told me? Perhaps I learned more by not staying. As I sit here now contemplating the meaning of that encounter, I feel that it altered the course of my existence. "You're not stupid", he said. He was telling me to awaken what I have inside and stop hiding from myself. . . stop looking for answers from others who do not know me like I know myself.*

For the two-hour drive back to Delhi airport, I sat in silence staring out into the night. I don't recall really seeing anything as we passed by. I was totally numb and in disbelief of the direction my life had taken. Miriam and I had been careful to not get too caught up in emotions as we said good-bye, especially me. I had done enough crying and letting go and wanted to be strong for the journey home. As I hugged her and wished her well, I felt her break, and watched as the tears streamed down her face. It was the most real emotion she had shown to me in weeks. We parted with hopeful words that we might one day find our way back, but deep in my heart I knew that this was the closing chapter for us.

Chapter Eight
Whatever it Takes

I waited in the airport at St. John's for Stefanie to come pick me up. As if in some surreal dream, it felt like I had left myself back in India and was only here physically. Turning to see Stefanie approaching brought a battle inside to not completely collapse in sheer emotional exhaustion. She offered me some nurturance and comfort over the next few days while I got my bearings back. My family didn't even know about my return because I wasn't ready to face their questions and looks of concern.

I had called Stefanie the same afternoon of descending from the mountains in India. She was the only person I felt that I could talk to. Even Daniel was at this point feeling removed from me. His e-mails carried energy of aloofness that I didn't understand. He didn't really support my relationship with Miriam and hadn't even come to our gathering to celebrate our send-off. So it didn't feel a good time to call him to report that maybe he had been right.

That first night out of the mountains, after I had made my decision to return, was horrible. It rained very heavily and the lightening had put out the power. The streets were pitch black and everything felt so eerie and gloomy. Miriam and I were not able to speak without tension or anger flaring up. I was feeling so completely alone. I stumbled through the rain and darkened streets to find a phone stand to call Stefanie. I told her what was happening and about plans to return home. She offered for me to stay with her and would honour my request not to tell anyone about my return. Now here I was in the airport thousands of miles away from those mountains and watching

Stefanie, my earthly guardian angel, coming to scoop me up from my flight home, just like the other angels of light that had assisted me on my path.

For the next month I went into some state of recluse, completely raw and stripped of any sense of my old self. I was, broke, homeless, and nowhere near emotionally ready to return to work. I meditated and continued to read my spiritual books, but it seemed like I had gone into a void where nothing was happening. Fears were setting in that my abilities to work with the energy were lost because the insightful dreams and visions weren't happening and everything felt really numb. My friends helped me out with places to stay and meals. The little bit of money I still had was dwindling fast. I felt so lost and uncertain and scared.

I realized the grave disservice I had done to Miriam, still carrying a flame for Kathleen while hoping Miriam could burn away that flame and replace it with her own. For whatever reason, I still loved Kathleen and continued to feel tortured by my desire to be with her.

Still

June 12, 2004

Through time and space

it has left its mark

like a branding iron

upon my heart.

I've been letting go

for so long now.

Still you are there.

Still it's your name

I hear whispered

in my dreams.

I tried to rekindle the friendship with Daniel but he had eased into the background after letting me have it for the stupid choices I had made. My motivation to care was gone from me so I wasn't able to really react against his outburst. He was acting from a place of concern and genuine caring, but no one outside of myself could truly understand the inner force that had driven me toward the choices that were made. I wasn't sure I understood it myself. Eventually Daniel and I were able to find our back and started to develop a more meaningful friendship of honesty and unconditional support.

As enticing as it was to return to work to have a cash flow, there was a recognition of not being prepared to jump back into my work as a Counsellor. The safe space nestled in my cocoon was needed a while longer. My grandmother bailed me out and gave me money to secure an apartment. It was very welcome to have my own private sanctuary. Once in a while I would venture out of my apartment for some fresh air. Driving to the beach was a ritual to spend long hours just staring out at the ocean, sitting on the rocks by the river, or on tree stumps in the forest; all the while absorbing any life energy that mother earth had to offer.

I eventually went back to work and tried to get back into the usual swing of things. A certain happiness came with re-connecting with everyone again, but I started to recognize that my real work was in my spiritual path, and in the energy healing that I had been doing. I was truly seeing beyond the world, and beyond what was happening on the surface of human experience. Everything was different now and it became unbearable to try to see things in the same way as before. I could no longer tolerate the little injustices and roles that were being played around me. Finally the courage came to resign from my career and devote my life to Spirit, taking a great leap into the unknown. I didn't realize it at the time, but I was taking a leap into another cycle of purging at an even deeper place inside of me.

"Pay attention to the synchronicities, surely they will come"
*message from my Guidance, **July 6, 2004***

I had awoken from a dreamtime lesson in which I was a little boy, standing on the edge of a pond with a man, a spiritual teacher. There was a pebble in my hand and it became the focus of the teaching he was giving me about having faith and patience. He talked about the importance of the seeds we plant in our lives. With a feeling of complete frustration, I threw the pebble into the water. He told me that faith in life was like the ripples produced by the pebble entering the water. When an upsetting event occurs, it's like the beginning of a process that with faith will send out ripples and eventually reach a greater calmness. He said that my faith are like those ripples, that all I have to do is believe and see the synchronicities, and that the results will manifest to teach others as well. In tossing that pebble, it was important to be aware of the intent placed into it so that its ripples would be produced from a place of love and not anger or frustration. I recognized this lesson as coming from a higher aspect of myself, and that little boy was my innocence and insecurity.

Over the course of the next year, I started receiving all sorts of messages in various forms. I was studying more intently *The Course in Miracles*, with Stefanie and Sam engaging me in many conversations and clarifying my questions. I slowly eased into *The Urantia Book: A Revelation for Humanity* and was astounded with my ability to grasp its content. It was exciting to be delving into the depths of the universe. My own intuition was sharpening along with developing a more intimate connection with my Guidance. Again old issues that I thought were gone came to the surface for release. This time around, I was going inward to the core of where all this had taken root. With my Guidance supporting me, I dove inward again for another leg of the journey toward wholeness. The unresolved conflicts would this time be released in love and acceptance.

Somewhere through the process of doing all the purging and cleansing of my life, of my old self, I made a commitment. I knew when leaving my career that my life was being dedicated to Spirit. Eventually, I made an even deeper dedication. One day I was sitting in the woods again, lost in myself and still going through a continued process of releasing and surrender. The peace and joy that waited for me was becoming more tangible. Spirit heard my commitment to go all the way and do whatever it takes to BE peace …whatever it takes.

I went through my continued trials and with each breath peeled away another layer of old stuff that no longer served me. Many people were questioning me on why I was allowing myself to suffer so much. My response was always the same; it was not suffering but a witnessing of the depths of joy and peace that was being offered to me. I received many confirmations of being honoured and loved. One day in particular I was feeling the weight of my struggle and looked up to the grey skies to ask for a sign. It didn't come immediately, but it did come.

Daniel and I were standing in his driveway after returning from a walk. The skies suddenly brightened and through an opening in the grey clouds, a stream of sunlight poured down. Behind the sunlight, the clouds were outlined with brilliant colors of a rainbow. I knew this was my sign. The same sign witnessed as a child, standing at the bus stop early one morning, watching these beams of sunlight pour down. Even at my young age, I somehow sensed that this was God's way of telling me that heaven waits. Here as an adult, I stood watching the sunbeams reach out to me again, filling me with renewed faith. It was a beautiful gift that I was happy to share with Daniel, who like me, had a deep appreciation for the little miracles.

Chapter Nine
And the Angels Sang

I willingly offered myself into the cleansing that was happening and with great faith embraced all the emotions and all the mirrors of myself that were presented. Some of these were difficult to face, but through my Guidance I continued to receive insights that helped me find my way. Dreamtime carried me away to receive my lessons and be given glimpses of the deep peace that was mine. A pathway was illuminated through what was happening in the world around me, with my family, my friends, and the world in general. I was developing a detachment from the unreal. Opportunities came to sort through embarrassment, shame, anger, and utter rawness of vulnerability, but with each new layer that was peeled away, blessings of the universe flowed in, and in essence, the blessings of my true self.

One of the most difficult lessons I still had to face was in the arena of relationships. For obvious reasons, there was a lot for me to mistrust about love relationships. In the span of only two years, I had lost a long-term relationship, fallen deeply for someone who was completely unavailable to me, and then allowed myself to get lost in another relationship so that it might save me from the love I was feeling for someone else. It always directed me back to having to face myself. For a time, my human desires played havoc on me, trying to cause me to rush into companionship again, but somehow I was able to keep my focus on what was real and started to see that part of the cleansing process was to purge all desires and misplaced affections. My dreams once again served as an arena to do this purging in a way that was safe and gentle for me.

"It's not some secret weapon that comes between nouns".
message from my Guidance, **September 21, 2004**

Dreamtime brought me to a number of intensely sexual dreams, some of them with individuals that I dearly loved and respected. Needless to say, these experiences were a little mortifying to me as fears crept up of the possible fall out from it. I had learned enough to know that the dreamtime is often where the truth reveals itself because it is here where the pureness of what is can be expressed. It disturbed me a great deal to see what my unconscious self was bringing up from my shadows. The strength and 'realness' of the exchange was astounding. Upon waking, I could still feel her in my arms and the weight of her body upon mine. As I wrapped my arms about myself, I was feeling her body not mine. This dream was so amazingly real that I was thrown in a stupor for days.

As much as I tried to push these dreams away, my attention kept being directed back to them again and again in order to face the emotions of it. A message that resonated with me after hearing it from Stefanie was "Let the meaningless data be replaced by my meaning". She had received this message from Universal Guidance and explained to me that it was referring to allowing the trueness of Spirit. I felt that the meaninglessness in these dreams needed to be recognized in order for me to see that there was a more real meaning to my dreams than what appeared through the disguise of the human sex drive. Despite my embarrassment, I found the courage to talk to Stefanie about it. I was so glad to receive a true confirmation of how real love transcends all form.

I began to understand what my Guidance was telling me, that real love isn't something that has to be secret. It is not something that gets used as a weapon in a perceived battle of special relationship. It was also telling me that love goes beyond words, beyond any need to have to say it in words out of a sense of expectation. Love is, pure and simple.

Stefanie looked at me and smiled saying, "just enjoy the feeling of it". What I experienced was a true communion that really had nothing to do with the physical act and everything to do with the oneness of being. She went on to tell me that it's the love that's real, not the story in which it's presented. In that moment, she showed me the most real and unconditional loving acceptance I had ever known. My courage to face what was coming up and to talk openly about it allowed me to embrace my further ascension into the real.

"Nothing you will ever see is hidden in Darkness".
message from my Guidance, **October 10, 2004**

With my brave exploration into my own identity as a sensual, sexual, creative being, I was able to reach into all those dark places of myself and bring it into the light. I understood what the message was telling me. In order to truly see the real, I had to bring all of it into the light. I had to embrace all aspects of myself, even those of judgment and of shame because it was all part of the illusion that needed to be shone away. I was in a process of balancing my energies and being centered.

October 21, 2004. What does achieving balance really mean? People often talk about trying to balance responsibilities, balance their time, or balance their sense of self. In striving to achieve a greater spirituality, it becomes easy to lose sight of the importance of balance. It starts to appear that you are only accomplishing something if you are doing, moving, going toward something, or if you can see visible changes happening. Growth also occurs in simply staying in the moment and being still, quiet, reflective, breathing and allowing Spirit to move through you. If you allow a simple state of being and empty yourself of expectations or perceptions of what should be happening, it is then that real change happens.

There is a time for movement and a time for staying still, such as the ebb and flow of tides. There is a still point in between where the rest occurs and strength gathers for the next movement to take place.

"You can enter here and in our sight"
message from my Guidance, **November 18, 2004**

The guards were coming down and allowing a freedom of expression that I couldn't muster before. One day after getting out of the shower and feeling really light-headed, I lay back on the bed and started thinking about the events of my life. For some quirky reason that I didn't understand at the time, I felt the need to lay there naked, asking for Spirit to receive me just as I had come into this world. I was again a naked baby with my layers of self-imposed identity stripped away. I felt completely vulnerable, yet free.

There was a feeling of complete resignation and acceptance in having no control over my life. I drifted into a meditative state and got carried through some sort of vortex. My physical body became extremely heavy and it seemed to sink down deeper into the bed beneath me. Then a wash of light sent tingling through my entire body. I was lifted gently into a light and then suddenly pulled like a vacuum was sucking me into a hole of some sort, a vortex.

On the other side, I met up with other beings of light and felt a powerful loving presence welcoming me. A male voice spoke so clearly to me, saying, "You can enter here, and in our sight". Upon hearing this, I snapped immediately back to my body and was fully alert.

That experience left me shaken for days, but in a good way. It was vindicating me in my doubts about whether I was on the right path. My communion with Spirit was calling me in many different forms. In many of the most seemingly mundane activities, a light was emanating to show me the thread of life force that connects us to everything. On occasion, when my intuition spoke to me, I offered card readings or angel messages to others. It always astounded me to feel the synchronicity of the messages being received through these instances. The joy in my heart for seeing the light of recognition shining in those around me was enough to burst me completely out of my seams. In offering Reiki or Cranio-Sacral sessions, an opening was created for light beings from the angelic realm to come in. It still blows me away to see these beautiful beings entering the sacred space to assist in treatments. It is such an honour to partake of this magnificent presence. It's unbelievable but at the same time so very believable because it's right there for my spiritual eyes to see.

The existence of angels wasn't a new concept for me, but to be experiencing for myself instead of through someone else's story was very new. Through all my birthing pains into my true self, angels and beings of light watched over me, guided me, and offered me reassurances. In meditations, the luminescent hands would reach out for me, many times showing me that the divine consciousness was also me, that I am God also. I had begun to reach a place of acceptance of my divinity and one day, in the middle of receiving some reiki energy through a friend's assistance, an angel spoke to me so clearly and lovingly saying, "Welcome Home". I looked up to see the radiant light of two hands reaching out for me. It was the same hands that had lifted me from the dark shadow that had descended on me in India. My heart again felt that it would literally explode with joy and love. In that moment I finally knew for real that I AM divine.

And the angels sang to me, gathering around me during treatment sessions and during meditations, offering healing, nurturance, and sometimes assisting me in sending intentions for healing to others. They started to become my friends, whom I could confide in and talk to about everything from the silly to the serious.

Around this time I was examining my connection to Daniel and asking for angelic assistance in understanding the human desires for connection. Daniel had supported me through the loss of my long-term relationship with Ana, my intense connection to Kathleen, my transition out of my old career, and even through my break up with Miriam. Over the past couple of years we seemed to mirror a great deal of each other's struggles and insecurities. At times I questioned the trueness of it, questioned whether it had become too safe and comfortable. For the time I was in India, it seemed that a distance had come between us, much of which was based on assumptions and misunderstandings. There was a point where I was beginning to feel that this friendship had run its course, but through it all, we saw the light in one another and continued to nurture it.

We have had many long hours of discussion and sharing our innermost thoughts and feelings and questions on the meaning of life. Daniel is a truly wonderful man, with a depth of spirit that I have rarely seen. We shared insights and in many ways inspired each other. Love came for this man, which in itself, seemed like a miracle to me. We often joked about the idea that if we were still single when we turned fifty, we would just marry and live a life together as companions. There were times in the midst of my heartache that I truly considered that idea. I was starting to truly see him for the first time, and began to more fully appreciate the compassion, acceptance, patience, and abiding love that he is.

I had for a time taken for granted the endless hours of support he'd given me, the countless small gestures of friendship. I realize now that I truly do love him, in a way that transcends all boundaries of form and limitation; not a romantic love, not a love that can be categorized or exploited. It serves as a strong affirmation of the soul connection that we as humans can share without having to judge it or box it into some restrictive expectation.

January 16, 2005. I'm not too certain at any given time what I'm supposed to be or where I am supposed to be heading. I feel lost and confused like never before. So often have I heard that I will be transformed; that just when I think I'm getting it, I will realize that I know nothing. That IS the truth. I started a long time ago writing a book, a script of what would be about my spiritual awakening. I'm seeing now that it is really a story about my death, of the many deaths along the way towards my true birth.

I heard the words, "God put you here as a woman to be with a man" For days, I carried the sick, empty feeling cutting away inside of me. I couldn't believe that such judgement came from the lips of someone I deeply trusted. My mind was full of questions and arguments against what this meant. I'm still not sure if I want to believe it, or accept it, or totally reject it. I don't know. I'm grasping at everything, anything to clear up this confusion and vindicate me in my desire to remain in the arms of a woman.

The past few months have brought many opportunities to let go and let God. I've reflected on all the changes and transformation and feel amazed at my life. I feel raw... so completely and utterly exposed and raw with emotions. I'm getting exactly what was asked for... true peace, my birthright... whatever it takes. I guess the warnings should have been heeded to be careful what I was asking for. At times, I'm thinking I am completely nuts.

January 17, 2005. I have heard so many times that cracking up is good because it allows a letting go. Well, I just cried my eyes out for about two hours, lost in a cloud of confusion and loneliness, praying for healing from whatever this is. Then looking over at my photo albums sitting on my shelf, it came to me what to do. I realized that I had been dragging around illusions for many years and it was now time to let go.

I spent the next couple of hours transforming my past by burning all my old photographs, and even the books that carried them. An intention was put into the flames to release me from everything that is no longer me. As I watched the images melt away into the flames, there was a certain sense of vindication because although I was a character in that production, I always felt outside of it. As the first photos were tossed into the fire, I prayed for release from all the energies that held me back; release from all the false ideas *and expectations of who I am supposed to be. I re-dedicated my trust in Spirit, that all is in perfect order. There were so many memories as I looked at faces, which even through their smiles, spoke of the unhappiness behind their eyes. All of them were characters in some unknown play, one that I was very much a part of, but no more. All those years of trying to capture a moment, of trying to capture a feeling or idea… I feel so strongly that that I no longer have any use for this illusion of me. At this moment, I am really not sure of who I am, but I trust that I will.*

I had for most of my life carried a feeling of not fully understanding my ability to be so deeply loving but never quite able to allow myself to be open to receive it. In the context of everything that I was learning about my identity as a fragment of God, I wanted to get to the bottom of this issue. Closer attention was given to the numerous insights and messages revealed to me over the last couple of years. The glimpses into my past life incarnations were calling me again. These glimpses had not come in any clear or consistent pattern, nor were they strong enough to determine if they were for real. Through a consultation with an Intuitive, the pieces fell into place. I finally reached some understanding of the powerful karmic influences over my emotions and prayed to the depths of my being for healing to come. My angels and even a little fairy friend from childhood stayed by my side in their continued vigilance. For a while, I floated on a high of the sense of freedom that came in releasing the past. Soon after it would become clear that this is only part of the clearing process to prepare for greater things, for showing me how much I didn't know.

One thing I did know, however, was that regardless of appearances of the package of love, my integrity in knowing who I am would be untouched. I don't need someone or something outside of me telling me to present my love in a certain form or package. Peacefulness settled over me in the knowledge of my inner wisdom for the karmic choices that brought me to where I am in this life. Still, the angelic choirs sing to me in recognition of my place in the divine.

Chapter Ten
A Lesson in Integrity

In my dedication to follow a spiritual life, I had unknowingly asked for great things to fall upon me. Spirit had heard my dedication and responded to it by offering me both a blessing and an opportunity to exercise my faith. Two teenagers came under my care, my sister Rebecca's children. As much as I wanted to scream out, "no I can't do this", something deep inside recognized the pull to follow this direction from Spirit. As I drove out to pick them up, a little voice inside was telling me that this was no ordinary day. The first few days would bring me a strong dose of having to stand my ground and not settle for less than what was deserved. I had to see beyond the system and speak to this on behalf of these kids with a voice that would exert strength and conviction. This became yet another trial that showed me more of myself and one that I would not fully appreciate until it had ended.

Trying to write about my experiences with these kids, I find it difficult to not get caught up in details of what happened. Maybe it's still too fresh for me; maybe I still hold on to some of the guilt for not being able to give them what I wanted to give them. It doesn't really matter what happened because what they needed wasn't up to me to decide. What matters is that at the core of this whole experience with them came an understanding of something very significant within myself. It was a big lesson in maintaining my integrity and seeing the importance of simply being the presence of peace.

I can laugh now, looking back, realizing the perfect timing of my lessons and appreciating how the universe offers opportunities for expansion. It was only a week or so prior to the kids moving in that I was listening to Raj's discussion on integrity. Listening to this particular discussion, somewhere inside I knew this would be my next lesson. As the words sank into my awareness my eyes rested on the evening sun casting its flashes of light through the leaves of the trees outside my window. Studying the leaves, one by one, issues that needed forgiveness were released into love. It all flowed together like a beautiful dance between lovers. My lover was becoming the essence of life itself. I felt ready to embrace the next lesson.

Michael and Jenny came to live with me after things fell apart at their dad's. They had a long life of turmoil. Rebecca's marriage to their dad subjected her and her four children to a great deal of conflict, abuse, and at times, even violence. After Rebecca left, they were subjected to more years of struggling, bitter custody battles, and continued violence. I have often remarked to my sister that I am truly amazed at the inner core of strength that she maintained through it all. For a young girl, pregnant at 17, married at 18 and a mother of four by the time she reached 25, Rebecca was nothing short of astounding. The turmoil she faced throughout her marriage and even years after she left would have driven many people to insanity. Not Rebecca. I hold great admiration for her strength and for the brilliant light that shines deep from within her soul to carry her through her trials. Like the song she sang as a child, the light was poured into her heart to offer her strength and direction. She has often remarked on the desire to have her four sweet and innocent kids back to make things different for them, but how could she possibly have known what would come of the choices they all made?

Michael was fourteen. He was a tiny scrap of a kid, who despite his tough attitude showed me a little boy that was hurting immensely. He was truly brilliant. He had great difficulty with his schoolwork but he made up for it in his intuitiveness, sharp wit, and ability to adapt quickly to whatever situation that presented. This was how he learned to survive. He announced very brazenly to me one day that he didn't have to ever worry about being hurt or in trouble because he could talk his way out of anything. Sometimes he would glare at people with his dark piercing eyes, so filled with anger and rage. He hated to be told what to do and resisted any and every hint of structure. Other times, even in the midst of his acting out, the tears would stream quietly over his cheeks and I would see glimpses of the lost, frightened little boy inside, trying desperately to control what was happening in his life. Sometimes the simplest surprises took him completely off guard and he didn't know what to do with it. It was easier for him to stay angry and mistrustful at the world than to show any vulnerability.

Jenny was a little older than her brother, soon to turn sixteen. She was soft spoken, except when she was really ticked off and could riddle off the curses and angry daggers as good as her brother could. She was deceptive because on the outside, she presented as quiet, accommodating, and accepting. Underneath was a raging sea of bitterness, anger, hurt, rejection, and confusion. She had learned to play the manipulation game in order to survive and went about trying to be the one who fixed everything for her friends. She was bright, caring, and insightful but never had enough belief in herself to really excel. For her, it was easier to go through the motions, not allowing any real feeling to come in.

On a daily basis, these kids caused me to face mirrors into myself. I looked into these faces, filled with so much anger, pain, and attitude against the world. There was a raging sea of feelings held back under a thin veil of smiles and nonchalance about their life. I looked beyond the guards and saw the innocent cries for help, for some sense of being loved, of belonging, and also of exerting their intuitiveness about what was right. It sang a very familiar tune to me and in some ways felt very scary. I wanted so much to offer help to these kids, to provide a buoy for them to cling to as they tried to find their way. I'd like to think that I did, even if they don't recognize it right now. Still, it was a great awakening for me.

We went through the daily rituals and routines, with them testing me in every way, just as all teenagers do to figure out their own sense of personal power. At first it seemed like it would all work out okay. We had our talks about learning to take good care of their bodies, recognizing how to make good choices about their friends and their life, and learning about making efforts to cooperate to make our new living accommodations bearable. Sometimes we had very insightful conversations about the deeper meaning of life. I learned a great deal from them. These kids were certainly not living under a rock. They had smarts, a way of seeing through the crap going on in the world. Once the initial newness of our arrangement sank in and they started to see me in the role of makeshift parent, that's when the trouble really started. They did not want to be parented, or controlled. They just wanted a smooth, free ride into adulthood.

Before too long, I began to feel the sense of being manipulated, taken for granted, disrespected, and in some ways, even abused. I was placed in the middle of a chaotic blend of illusions, emotional games, control tactics, and a social system that was not being real. It was a perfect opportunity to practice being in my peace. As much as I recognized the truth in what was happening, I felt myself slowly crumbling under the weight of the issues they brought out.

I allowed the game to continue a while longer, still doing what I could to set some things right, but soon the reality would show me that I had no control over any of this. Then came the realized that it wasn't about them at all, it was about me. It was an opportunity to exercise my faith and maintain my integrity. Once this clarity came, I knew immediately that it was time to stand my ground, exert my position, and re-claim my peace.

That last week of us still living together was extremely tense and difficult. There was conflict all around us. Michael had really started acting out and becoming more volatile with each passing day. There was nothing I could do to save him from the self-destructive ways of hurting his body and his relationships. On the other side, Jenny would start acting out with her moods and unrealistic demands. It was a continuous bombardment of teenage angst and struggles for power and control. As much as I wanted to remain calm, loving, and nurturing, there was acknowledgement of needing this more for myself. The events naturally unfolded. Throughout that week, my integrity was tested in numerous ways, but I remained firm in my conviction that I was doing what was right for me. I made the calls to have them removed from my care.

For about a week after they moved out, I went into a state of complete despair, crying for days to release all the sorrow, the disappointment, and the agony over having not helped them, questioning what would face them, and knowing that my actions had set of a chain reaction of events for them. Still, I did recognize that it really had nothing to do with me. They had to make their own choices. It is not my place to teach them lessons. It is only my place to see the lessons in it for myself.

I also cried for the trauma it had put me through, quite literally nursing my wounds like someone who had been through a battering. For several days, feeling absolutely drained of energy or desire to do anything, I became a couch potato and tuned out from the world. I was physically ill and so weak that trying to crawl up off the couch only resulted in a collapse on the floor. My heart cried out with longing to have a partner to hold me and comfort me as I went through this, but it was something I would have to learn to do for myself. My woollen shawl was wrapped around me and nestled me in front of a fire glowing in my fireplace. As always, the gentleness of the love of Spirit settled around me to nurture me back to myself.

Daniel called on a daily basis to encourage and motivate me. He had seen me through a great deal of the turmoil with the kids, giving me some direction as to dealing with the system in which I relied to support me in giving care to these kids. He was a voice of wisdom and experience. When I spoke to my friend Stefanie of feeling very much like a couch potato she reminded me that when potatoes are left long enough they start to sprout little flowers. Once again, she showed me the beauty in every experience.

My apartment seemed to be grieving as well. The air felt heavy with the remaining tension and gloominess of what had just unfolded, as well as holding the tears and sadness I was releasing. I eventually found my way back to myself and then went through my apartment, re-arranging furniture, using sweet grass and white sage to smudge away the spent energies. My space was re-claimed as a peaceful, light-filled space. Beyond that, I had no idea what I was going to do.

So I went back to my life with some reservations after putting everything on hold in order to care for the kids. My healing work was at a seeming standstill and very little had been happening in regards to workshops and gatherings. It shouldn't have been surprising, though, considering the tension and conflict that I had been immersed into. It seemed that every effort to create a flow in my work was dampened by this cloud of conflict that surrounded me.

One bright spot had been a film release that I was fortunate to host. It was the world premiere release of "Indigo", a film about psychic and highly intuitive children. It provided me with an outlet for some of my attention while the pieces of the home arrangement came apart. It's funny, though, because here I was living and breathing the dynamics of caring for two troubled teens while introducing the concept of Indigo to groups of people who had never heard of it. Again, the universe showed me a taste of how Divine Timing operates to provide the ideal experience at the very moment when it would be most real.

Once the space in my apartment was re-claimed, along with my heart space, it seemed that all of my co-creations toward my perfect peace were bearing fruit. All the threads of my being were drawing closer to my coming into my true self. I was completing a cycle and feeling free. I felt the overwhelming sense that "it is done", my graduation from a huge piece of my waking up and of clearing my soul of old energy and of old karma. I made peace with myself, and in the process, made peace with that beautiful soul, Kathleen, who had triggered my whirlwind journey into my own heart. I truly felt that I had turned a corner.

Chapter Eleven
The End of the Beginning

As meaningful as it all was, it no longer exists except as some memory of a journey for someone who is no longer me. I have to let it go and accept that my true learning has only just begun. Thinking back over my journey, I don't even recognize me anymore. Again there has been a shift in perception and a transformation that has brought me to new awareness. I realize that this story is just that…a story.

Messages have been finding their way to me over the past several weeks. These messages come in various forms. One day I happened to turn on the radio just in time to hear songs talking of entering heaven. At that precise moment, I knew it was telling me that I am on the verge of truly entering heaven, which in reality is the divinity within me that wants to shine forth and let go of the perceptions of who Nancy thinks she is. The songs continued to give me messages of being rich in Spirit and having riches beyond money or material things. Having been in a place of worrying about my financial obligations, these songs were telling me to trust in Spirit because I was already rich in the eyes of the universe. It was up to me to get out of the way to allow this abundance to flow in.

In reading *The Matrix Warrior*, written by Jake Horsley, another realization came that I was in a dangerous place; dangerous in the sense that I had allowed myself to think that I had figured it out. Not so. A true enlightenment comes with a realization of still being a student, and with realizing the mastery of the emotions. I am not there yet. I am still very much a student needing to temper my ego and my Higher Wisdom.

I was having a conversation with Stefanie about how asking Spirit to speak through us means becoming completely empty and getting ourselves out of the way. She referred to it as letting go of the story. In other words, there is no story; there is only this very moment. Nothing else exists. So here I am again, reviewing all that I have written about my story and realizing that it no longer exists. Sure, it's a great read and perhaps someone reading it will feel inspired or motivated, but for me as the person identified in the personality of this story, she no longer exists.

Three months have passed since I had written what I thought would be the closing remarks of my book. Part of me felt like scrapping the whole thing because I recognized how much illusion is wrapped up in this story. I actually think it's laughable when I see the mixed up emotions and perceptions that weaved through all this. What was I thinking?!

I was starting to understand the concept of ACIM which explained how we create a meaningless world from meaningless thoughts. In other words, everything that this story tells of my experiences is nothing more than manifestations of the projected emotions and false ideas about the meaning of my existence. My life, as with many people's lives, has been a course lesson in undoing the illusion and uncovering the stuff that has obscured my true Being. I don't mean to sound nonchalant about the story because it was very important in its purpose, but the moment has passed, at least for me. Still, some part of me wants to share it because I know how much growth came for me in these experiences. Perhaps it can come for those who read about it.

Many opportunities have presented to me over the past several weeks to go deeper into my peace. I have been confronted and challenged in numerous ways that tested my integrity and shaken me from my false perceptions. I've come to realize how much I still don't know.

I was reading *Friendship With God* about a month ago and something really stood out. Neale Donald Walsch had been asking God about why he had gone through certain experiences. God's reply was that we are given experiences in order to learn from them and share our growth with others in order to help them also shine their light. So I decided to not scrap this story. I hope that it was the right choice.

I'm coming through another period of being really messed up in my thinking. I've been pulled in many directions and feeling really confused about the direction my life is taking. The universe gave me a wonderful gift of having a beautiful house to look after for a few weeks. It was truly a quiet sanctuary, an awesome blessing offered to me by two trusting souls. I spent my days sitting in a sun-filled meditation room or in the front garden listening to the breeze rustling the leaves of the trees. Endless hours were spent simply sitting, reflecting, and tuning out from the world. Time seemed to stand still as I again found some peace inside.

I went for a walk in the park yesterday. It was the first time in a couple of weeks that I had given myself the time to breathe. I had again become caught up in the conflict and the ideas that I could control how my life was unfolding. Questioning my purpose and the purpose for being inspired to write this manuscript, I had reaching a point of really wanting to scream. I needed air and started spending all my time walking through the park and along the river where I would dangle my feet just as I had done as a child. My attention again was drawn into watching the shadows of current reflected off the river bottom. Breathing in the fragrant air of blossoming trees and watching the leaves flutter in the breeze, I knew God was speaking to me. Climbing up a large oak tree reminded me of how much time I had spent as a child climbing high into the sky. Lying back along one of the branches, feeling totally supported by the tree, I closed my eyes and allowed the energy of the tree to fill me. My tensions melted away and took with it the massive headache I had been carrying. This is a glimpse of what life is really about. I used to laugh when I heard stories about the tree-huggers, thinking how silly it was. Now I understand the power and peace that comes from allowing the life force of Mother Earth to connect with me. I'm very happy to be a tree-hugger.

As I walked along the river trail, I felt tears, sorrow, loneliness, and then a quiet calming peace settling in. I'm not really sure what I was crying for, only that it followed a need to release whatever it was. Sometimes my heart still feels the ache for those who have touched my heart so deeply. Ana is a distant memory although I have spoken with her on occasion and we have released the blame. I made my peace with Miriam, too, offering my heartfelt blessing for her happiness. Kathleen had given me such a beautiful gift, an opportunity to exercise my integrity. The ache in my heart for her is no longer about a misplaced affection. It is for the recognition of the powerful and deep lessons she mirrored for me. For so long I felt intimated by her, but I am now able to see her through truth as my equal. As much I might wish that there could have been friendship between us, for whatever reason, we still can't seem to make our peace. Maybe one day we will.

My day in the park served as a review for me, with every step letting go of memories and the story of my life thus far. My thoughts went back to several months ago when I attended a Reiki retreat. The second morning there, I felt the need to opt out of the morning meditation with the group. That was unusual for me because I had always been one to not want to miss out on anything. I went instead to the cliffs overlooking the ocean and had my conversation with God, asking for direction. In a clear voice I heard the message "The time has come". I wasn't entirely certain what this meant but I knew my life was about to take a drastic turn for the better. So here I was now, walking through the park, letting go, and asking for direction once again. I realized the time had come for the closing of this story.

I meditated under a rhododendron tree, drinking in the violet and green colors and the golden rays of the sun shining on the leaves. Entering into that stillness, I felt more peaceful than I had in weeks. It brings me back to remembering that I do not need to worry about what to do or how to be. All I need do is allow the stillness to settle in and listen for direction from Spirit.

In recent days, I have been called upon in ways I didn't expect but it has been very rewarding to my soul. I've been in the company of beautiful people needing to drink up some of the peace they see in me. Little do they know how much my soul has been quenched by their beauty. Last night I spent some quality time with my dear friend Sam. He again helped me to remember that I am exactly where I am supposed to be, that I am living my purpose by simply allowing the emergence of who I truly am.

So now I sit here in this chair, typing on this computer, reading these words, remembering to breathe, and coming back to that place of quiet within my own heart.

Epilogue

I'm sitting here today, writing the last thoughts that will clue up this story. I've been glued to my computer for days, not being able to tear myself away from my own story. This journey so far has left me feeling enthralled, amazed, inspired, and sometimes even flabbergasted by my own experiences. I have laughed. I have cried. I have felt stunned and astounded. I have also felt the profound joy. Having sifted through the aspects of my life, it brought many reminders of the gratitude for where I am and for who I am. I can see my life now through the eyes of Spirit and recognize that it is infused with the pure love of Spirit.

Scanning over the years of pain and hurt inside myself and in relation to my family and friends, I can truthfully say that I have grown beyond it. Somehow, the tiny little girl who was always so shy and reserved has blossomed into a light shining into the world. I can step out in full presence of my authentic self, no longer feeling like putting on a show or having sadness of the moment of glory coming to an end. Every moment is glorious in the presence of my BEING. I have reached a beautiful place of acceptance of all that I meet, especially my family, whom I have come to cherish in a whole new way.

I am not so arrogant as to portray myself as having it all figured out because this learning curve is quite large. There's a recognition that Spirit has led me through a time of purification in which I was a willing participant. The beauty of this life of Spirit is that it is in constant fluidity of releasing and surrendering and embracing. I am at every moment given the opportunity for expansion inward, into the imaginal of the universe.

The real journey has only just begun.

From humble beginnings come great things. It is the greatest, most profound journey. It is a journey that unseen to the commoner, leaves a lasting impression upon its participants. And so it truly begins...

I share with you my light so that you may see it in yourself.

Reference List

A Course In Miracles. Mill Valley, CA: Foundation For Inner Peace, 1992.

Carroll, Lee and Tober, Jan. **The Indigo Children**. Carlsbad, CA: Hay House Inc., 1999.

Chodron, Pema. **When Things Fall Apart: Heart Advice For Difficult Times**. Boston: Shambala Publications, 1997.

Coelho, Paulo. **The Alchemist**. Australia: Harper Collins, 1993.

Demartini, Dr. John F. **The Breakthrough Experience.** Carlsbad, CA: Hay House, Inc., 2002.

Gregg, Levoy. **Callings: Finding and Following an Authentic Life**. New York: Three Rivers Press, 1997.

Hay, Louise L. **You Can Heal Your Life**. Carlsbad, CA: Hay House Inc., 1999.

Horsley, Jake. **The Matrix Warrior: Being The One**. New York: St. Martin's Press, 2003.

Klein, Marc. **Serendipity**. New York: Miramax Films, 2001.

Laflamme, Lise. **The Wonder of Rainbows**. Spain: Vesica Piscis, 2000.

McCormack, Pete. **The Blue Butterfly**. Monterey Media Independent Films, 2004..

McGraw, Dr. Phil. **Self Matters: Creating Your Life From the Inside Out**. New York: Simon & Schuster Inc., 2001.

Morgan, Marlo. **Mutant Messages Down Under**. New York: Harper Perennial, 1991.

Myss, Caroline. **Anatomy of the Spirit**. New York: Three Rivers Press, 1996.

Myss, Caroline. **Sacred Contracts: Awakening Your Divine Potential**. New York: Three Rivers Press, 2002.

Prophet, Mark L. and Prophet, Elizabeth Clare. **The Science of the Spoken Word**. Corwin Springs, MT: Summit University Press, 1965.

Ragusa, Moreah. **Our Cosmic Dance**. Okotoks, AB: Phoenix Coaching and Transformation Corporation, 2004.

Redfield, James. **The Celestine Prophesy**. New York: Warner Books, 1993.

Redfield, James. **The Tenth Insight: Holding the Vision**. New York: Grand Central Publishing, 1998.

Redfield, James. **The Secret of Shambhala**. New York: Bantam Books, 2000.

Renard, Gary. **The Disappearance of the Universe**. Carlsbad, CA: Hay House, Inc., 2002.

Riso, Don Richard and Hudson, Russ. **Personality Types**. Boston: Houghton Mifflin Company, 1996.

Roberts, Jane. **Seth Speaks**. Toronto: Bantam Books, 1972.

Roberts, Jane. **The Nature of Personal Reality**. Toronto: Bantam Books, 1974.

Shakespeare, William. **As You Like It**. London: Oxford University Press, 1914.

The Urantia Book: A Revelation For Humanity. Chicago: Uversa Press, 1996.

Tolle, Eckhart. **A New Earth: Awakening to Your Life's Purpose**. New York: Penguin Group, 2005.

Tolle, Eckhart. **The Power of Now**. Mumbai, India: Yogi Impressions, 2001.

Twyman, James F. **Emissary of Love: The Psychic Children Speak to the World**. Charlottesville, VA: Hampton Roads Publishing Co. Ltd, 2002

Twyman, James F. **Praying Peace**. Forres, Scotland: Findhorn Press, 2000

Walsh, Neale Donald. **Friendship With God**. New York: G.P. Putnam's Sons, 1999.

Walsh, Neale Donald. **The New Revelations: A Conversation With God**. New York: Atria Books, 2002.

Williamson, Marianne. **Return To Love**. New York, Harper Perennial, 1992.

Vanzant, Iyanla. **One Day My Soul Opened Up**. New York: Simon & Schuster, 1998.

ISBN 978-142690244-4